The RED BLAZER GIRLS

THE Secret Cellar

Michael D. Beil

A Yearling Book

Text copyright © 2012 by Michael D. Beil
Cover art and interior illustrations copyright © 2012 by Daniel Baxter

All rights reserved. Published in the United States by Yearling, an imprint of Random House Children's Books, a division of Random House, Inc., New York. Originally published in hardcover in the United States by Alfred A. Knopf, an imprint of Random House Children's Books, New York, in 2012.

Yearling and the jumping horse design are registered trademarks of Random House, Inc.

Visit us on the Web! randomhouse.com/kids

Educators and librarians, for a variety of teaching tools, visit us at RHTeachersLibrarians.com

The Library of Congress has cataloged the hardcover edition of this work as follows:
Beil, Michael D.
The Red Blazer Girls : the secret cellar / by Michael D. Beil. — 1st ed.
p. cm.
Summary: When Sophie finds a secret message in the antique fountain pen she bought for her father, she and her friends become involved in a treasure hunt devised by the pen's previous owner, whose house is full of puzzles that protect a hidden treasure.
ISBN 978-0-375-86741-5 (trade) — ISBN 978-0-375-96741-2 (lib. bdg.) — ISBN 978-0-375-89790-0 (ebook) — ISBN 978-0-375-86495-7 (tr. pbk.).
[1. Mystery and detective stories. 2. Puzzles—Fiction. 3. Buried treasure—Fiction.
4. Eccentrics and eccentricities—Fiction. 5. Christmas—Fiction. 6. Catholic schools—Fiction. 7. Schools—Fiction.] I. Title. II. Title: Secret cellar.
PZ7.B3882345Red 2012 [Fic]—dc23 2011051981
Printed in the United States of America
10 9 8 7 6 5 4 3 2 1

First Yearling Edition 2013

Random House Children's Books supports the First Amendment and celebrates the right to read.

What's this? *Another* secret message?

For the Dominican Sisters of SVF

Chapter 1

One does not argue with Fate, the Red Blazer Girls Code, or Andrew Jackson

I'm peeking through an opening in the threadbare velvet curtain that leads into the tiny storefront parlor of Madame Zurandot, who, according to the flashing neon sign in the window, is both PSYCHIC! *and* CLAIRVOYANT! Two of my fellow wearers-of-the-red-blazer, Rebecca Chen and Leigh Ann Jaimes, look over my shoulders and nudge me inside.

"I can't believe we're doing this. Maybe it's not such a good—" I say as four hands give me a final push. A combination of smells, none of them particularly pleasant, greets me: vanilla incense, mothballs, and, somewhere in the distance, slow-cooking cabbage. Before me is a small round table that looks exactly as I had imagined it would. Seriously, Madame Zurandot has a crystal ball.

"Can I help you?" a voice asks from behind another curtain.

Gulp.

• • •

Ten minutes earlier, the three of us had been enjoying a chilly December Saturday in Manhattan, doing a little Christmas shopping and dreaming of the long school vacation, just two weeks away. On most Saturdays, Leigh Ann (the beautiful, graceful one) had dance class and Becca (talented, artistic) had art lessons, but they were both on break until January. Only Margaret Wrobel (genius, absolute best friend in the world) had plans; besides being the smartest person I know, she's also a future violin superstar and takes lessons from my mom every Saturday, rain or shine, vacation or no vacation.

I spotted it first, a microsecond before Rebecca but enough to beat her to it. Lying there on the sidewalk in front of Madame Zurandot's, folded neatly in fourths, was a twenty-dollar bill!

"Well, hello, Mr. Jackson," I said, unfolding it and holding it up to make sure it was the genuine article.

"Sophie St. Pierre, you are the luckiest person I know," said Leigh Ann. "I don't think I've ever found a quarter."

"What should we do with it?" I asked. "I mean, it's found money. We have to spend it."

"You could buy lunch," Rebecca suggested. "I'm getting hungry."

Leigh Ann shook her head. "No, you should spend it on something for yourself. Or for Raf."

Raf—as in Rafael Arocho—is my boyfriend-who-I'm-not-allowed-to-call-a-boyfriend-until-I'm-sixteen.

"No, no, no," protested Rebecca. "Absolutely not. The rules in this situation are clear: if you find money when you're with other Red Blazer Girls, the money must be shared."

"What rules?" Leigh Ann asked. "You're making that up."

"Actually, she's right," I admitted. "And it's even my rule. Last summer, before you started hanging out with us, I found a five in the park one day—"

"What! You found a five, and now a twenty! That is *so* not fair," said Leigh Ann.

I shrugged. "I can't help it. It just . . . happens. But I told Margaret and Becca that it was only right to share. The Red Blazer Girls Code, I guess."

"I have an idea," said Becca, pointing at the sign in Madame Zurandot's window. "First visit, twenty dollars. It's fate. We have to do it."

"A psychic? Are you crazy?" I said.

"What, you don't believe in them?" Becca asked.

"I, uh, no. Yeah, no. I mean, I'm not sure. Margaret says it's a bunch of hooey."

"Oh, jeez. I should have known," Becca scoffed. "So what if Miss Scientific Method doesn't believe. How often do you have a chance like this? Even Margaret would have to admit that having twenty bucks just drop

3

out of the sky the exact moment that you're standing in front of a sign that says FIRST CONSULTATION $20 is just . . . I mean, what are the odds?"

I had to admit, she had something there.

"Okay, but we don't tell Margaret. She'd be so disappointed."

"You have a serious problem," said Becca.

I didn't disagree.

A young woman—twenty at most, and dressed in jeans and a Lady Gaga T-shirt—appears from behind the curtain. Not at all what I'm expecting from a psychic. But then, maybe she knew that, and changed into those clothes just to catch me off guard. Pret-ty darn clever, these psychics.

"Hi," I say. "I, er, we were wondering if we could, you know, get a, um, reading. But if you're not . . . ready, we can come back later."

"Oh, yer lookin' for ma," she says, laughing. "She's the psychic. Have a seat. I'll get her for ya." She goes back through the curtain. "Ma! Ya got cust-a-muz!"

My eyes dart nervously from Becca to Leigh Ann to the ominous-looking crystal ball as we wait for Madame Zurandot.

"You should go first, Becca," I say. "It was your idea."

"Yeah, but you found the money," she says. "And I don't think she's going to tell all our fortunes for twenty bucks."

The curtain parts again and, following a dramatic pause, Madame Zurandot glides into the room as if she's on roller skates. (She's wearing a peasant skirt that drags on the floor, so, for all I know, she might actually be wearing skates.)

Without a word, she takes my fingers into her own cold, chapped hands and stares straight into my eyes for a full ten seconds without blinking. Then she closes her eyes and says, in an accent that I can't place, "I see a black dog running across an open field. You are trapped in a small room. And an old man with a cane, a man who is not who you thought he was, stands before a blue door with the number nine on it. And I see romance. . . . But wait! I see an enemy who becomes a friend, and a friend who becomes an enemy."

Okay, I'll admit it: I am freaking out as she finally breaks away from me and roughly grabs Leigh Ann's hands.

"Someone you love—someone who is far, far away—is waving to you from a boat. You are kneeling on a cold stone floor in the dark, searching for something that has been hidden away for many years. A girl in a red coat hands you a message. . . . I see the letters, but I'm afraid I cannot read the words; it is in a language I do not understand."

Rebecca's turn. Madame Zurandot takes her hands into her own and squeezes so hard that Becca opens her eyes wide. "You are standing alone in the midst of great beauty—a museum, perhaps. There is a single window on one wall, and when you look through it, you see a dead man, facedown at his desk, his pen still in his hand."

She drops Becca's hands and slumps down into a chair, her eyes closed and palms flat on the table.

The three of us stand there for a long time, waiting for her to say or do something. It's getting awkward, and just as I'm about to clear my throat to remind her that we're still in the room, she suddenly blurts out, "Others seek the same treasure you do, and though your quest may become dangerous, you must not give up. Be careful who you trust."

She opens her eyes and looks up at us, her face expressionless. "And that is all I see."

"Ummm . . . yeah," Becca says. "About those things you saw. Are those all things from the past? Or are they things that haven't happened yet?"

One corner of Madame Zurandot's mouth turns up into a half smile. "That is a question I cannot answer. Perhaps you will find more money on the sidewalk another day and you will return."

I feel my mouth fall wide open. "Wait. How did you—"

"Duh. She's psychic," says Becca, earning herself a slug in the arm.

"Look to the stars," adds Madame Zurandot mysteriously. "The answers are in the stars."

• • •

"So, do you still think it's a bunch of hooey?" Becca asks as we start back uptown. "She totally nailed it. The dog, the man with the cane, looking for something under a stone floor—it's like she knows everything we've done for the past three months. She's like Galadriel."

Leigh Ann and I share a look, our faces blank. "Who?"

Becca, who is obsessed with *The Lord of the Rings*, shakes her head sadly at us. "Remember? She's the one who makes Frodo look into her mirror, which is really just a big bowl of water, but it's where he sees the future. Except it might not be the future if he can destroy the ring. Jeez, do you guys pay attention at all?"

"It *was* kind of creepy," Leigh Ann admits. "That thing she said about someone I love waving at me from a boat? My dad just emailed me a picture of himself in Cleveland, and guess where he was standing. On a boat. Some guy he knows recently bought it."

"Wh-what about the dead guy she saw? Facedown at his desk, his creepy, twisted fingers still gripping his pen. That definitely hasn't happened yet," I note. "Has it? Or this blue door with the number nine on it."

Becca grins mischievously. "Maybe, maybe not. I would tell you, but Madame Z. said not to trust anybody. So, where to next? I'm really hungry."

Leigh Ann throws her arm around my shoulders.

"Hey, Soph, is your dad home today? Why don't we just go there for lunch? Maybe he could make us some of those croque-sandwichy-things again. That way we can save some money . . . and then, see, you could buy him an even nicer Christmas present. We would be helping him, in a way."

My dad is French, and the chef in a downtown restaurant—the kind of place grown-ups go for birthdays and anniversaries—and from Leigh Ann's first bite of his fabulous, Frenchified version of mac 'n' cheese, she has been trying to figure out a way to have my parents adopt her.

"Sorry, he's out at some winery on the North Fork. A couple of his friends from when he was a kid just started working there."

"I vote for pizza," Becca says.

"Big surprise there," I snort.

"It's the perfect food," she replies. "Bread, vegetables, dairy—"

"Yeah, yeah. Heard it before. Fine. Can we at least go to Luciano's? Their slices are better than our usual places. They're almost as good as Trantonno's."

"And the guys who work there are cuter," Leigh Ann notes.

"Really? I hadn't noticed," I lie.

That, of course, doesn't get past Becca. "You are such a liar, Sophie. When we were in there last week, you couldn't take your eyes off that kid with the bright blue eyes. The one who gave you the free garlic knots."

I fight off the biological urge to blush. "You're crazy. He's like sixteen years old!"

"And besides, she has Raf," says Leigh Ann. She pauses, smiling mischievously at Becca. "And Nate."

Becca gives her a high five. "Nice one, L.A."

I'd better explain about Nate, because it's not what you're thinking. In the Red Blazer Girls Detective Agency's last case, in between getting my nose broken by Livvy Klack and solving the mystery of the Mistaken Masterpiece, I was Nate Etan's dog-sitter. Yes, that Nate Etan—and, yes, I still have his private cell phone number and email address. (And, no, you can't have them.) While it is true that my spending all that time with a big movie star did make the previously mentioned Raf just a teensy bit jealous, that's all in the past, and Raf and I are just fine now, thank you very much. The boy with those remarkable, sparkling-blue eyes at Luciano's? Hey, I was just being friendly. New York is, after all, the friendliest city in the world.

Back in my neighborhood, the East Nineties, Margaret meets us at the pizza shop, where, sadly, Blue Eyes has the day off. Becca and Leigh Ann are determined to tell her about our Madame Zurandot experience, even though I beg them not to. I'm outvoted, though, so all I can do is listen, cringing at every cheesy detail, and wait for Margaret to scold us for wasting twenty bucks on a psychic.

But the new and improved, open-minded Margaret just listens and laughs. "I'm sorry I missed that," she says, and I think she even means it.

"So, wait a second," I say. "You believe in psychics?"

"I never said that. I just wish I'd been there to see the looks on your faces when she said all that stuff."

"But what about what she said?" Leigh Ann asks.

Margaret shrugs. "It's interesting, but it still doesn't make me believe that she's really psychic. There's always another explanation. She could have recognized you guys from one of the stories in the paper about us. Or it could all just be a coincidence."

From the pizza shop, we walk down to Eighty-First Street, where there's a used-book store that Margaret wants to check out. With Christmas just around the corner, we decided to pool our money to buy a small present for our English teacher, Mr. Eliot. After all, this whole Red Blazer Girls thing got started in his classroom the day I saw Elizabeth Harriman's face in the church window, and even Becca (who is certain that he doesn't like her) has to admit that he's been a huge help to us. Since he's kind of—no, he's seriously—obsessed with Charles Dickens, we're looking for an old copy of one of Dickens's books, something a little more interesting than your basic paperback.

Before I tell you about the bookstore, however, there's something I have to confess: I absolutely love Manhattan in December. A few days after Thanksgiving, tens of thousands of pine trees miraculously spring up from the sidewalks overnight, courtesy of an army of French-Canadian Christmas tree farmers. I will go blocks out of my way to walk through the "forests," slowing down to fill my lungs with air that, for a change, isn't half carbon monoxide. For a few precious weeks, New York actually smells wonderful. (Now there's something you don't hear every day.)

The bookstore is so tiny that we're almost past it when we see the sign painted on the door:

STURM & DRANG BOOKS
RARE EDITIONS BOUGHT AND SOLD
MARCUS KLINGER, PROPRIETOR

One of those old-fashioned bells jangles when we go inside. The shop is maybe ten or twelve feet wide, and it is crammed—floor to ceiling, front to back—with old books, giving it that distinctive dusty-old-book smell, which is, to me, right up there with the scent of the pine forests along Second Avenue.

Standing on the third step of an antique brass and wood ladder is a middle-aged man, mostly bald, peering at us over a pair of reading glasses. Because he's up so high, it's hard to tell just how tall he is, but he seems to be well over six feet, with long, birdlike arms and legs.

"May I help you?" he asks, shelving the book he was reading. Not exactly friendly (which is what I expect of a bookstore owner), but not obviously hostile, either.

Leigh Ann, Becca, and I are suddenly struck mute, and look to Margaret to take charge, which she acknowledges with a sad shake of her head.

"Hi, yes, I hope so," she says. "We're looking for a gift for our English teacher. He's a huge fan of Charles Dickens, so we were hoping to find a nice old copy of *Great Expectations* or maybe *A Tale of Two Cities*. But we're open to other ideas if you don't have either of those."

The man climbs down from the ladder without a word and moves to an eye-level shelf in the center stack, from which he removes a single book.

He opens the cover, beautifully bound in coffee-colored leather, and turns to us. "Do you have a budget in mind?"

We look at Margaret, and I'm sure we're all thinking the same thing: please don't say something crazy, like a hundred bucks. I mean, I *do* like Mr. Eliot, but let's be reasonable.

"Um . . . twenty or twenty-five dollars?" she says.

"Twenty would be good," I say.

The man—MARCUS KLINGER his name badge says—sighs loudly and returns the book to its place on the shelf. "I see." He moves to another shelf and pulls down a thin volume. "I have this copy of *A Christmas Carol*—I assume you've heard of it. It's forty dollars, but I could let you have it for thirty-five. That's the best I can do."

"Can I see it?" Margaret asks.

Another sigh as he holds out the book. "Your hands are clean?"

Margaret glares at him, horrified, before snatching it from his hands.

He doesn't apologize; in fact, he seems completely oblivious. "Gilt edge. Calf binding. It's a reprint, an American edition, of course. A bargain at thirty-five dollars."

Margaret hands it back to him. "We'll think about it." She takes me by the arm and practically drags me out the door, with Becca and Leigh Ann on our heels.

"Man, what a loser," Becca announces as the door slams shut behind her.

"I was gonna call him something a lot worse than that," says Leigh Ann. "We have a word for people like him in Queens." She pauses, then continues, smiling to herself, "Actually, we have a lot of words for people like that."

"Tell me he didn't really ask you if your hands were clean," I say.

"Oh, he asked, all right," Margaret says. "And if that book is worth thirty-five dollars, I'm Cleopatra, queen of the Nile. It's a cheap knockoff that you can find any-where for seven ninety-nine."

"Begging your paaaardon, miss," says Becca, mocking Mr. Klinger. "That's a genuine turtle-skin binding. The paper was made from leftover bits of wood from Noah's ark, and the ink was brewed from a baby bald eagle's blood."

"What kind of names are 'Sturm' and 'Drang,' anyway?" Leigh Ann asks, looking back at the door. "I wonder which one he was."

"They're not names," says Margaret. "It's German. It means 'storm and stress.' I think Goethe—he was a German writer—was involved somehow."

"And you know this . . . how? Let me guess: the Harvard Classics. Right?"

"Naturellement."

Margaret is the proud owner of the complete set of the Harvard Classics, also known as Dr. Eliot's Five-Foot Shelf. Apparently, this Dr. Eliot guy (no relation to our Mr. Eliot) was the president of Harvard but used to tell people that all the books they really needed to be a well-educated person could fit on a five-foot shelf. (Why, then, are people so obsessed with getting into Harvard? I mean, their own president basically admitted that no one needs to go there. Kinda makes you think, doesn't it?) One of Margaret's (many, many) goals is to read every word—and we're talking about a collection of books that includes a whole volume called *Prefaces and Prologues*. Thrilling stuff, I'm sure. Right up there with

14

Glossaries I Have Loved and *The Year's Best Tables of Contents*.

"Well, we can take a trip down to the Strand after school one day next week and look for Mr. Eliot's book there," I say. "They have everything, and they're not going to try to scam us. And besides, I have a list of books I want to buy, but can't afford them all if I get new ones."

"Or you could go to the library, like a normal person," says Margaret, who accuses me of having a compulsive book-buying disorder.

"You know, I don't think I've ever walked down this street before," I say. "Look at all those little shops on the other side. Let's go check them out—maybe I can find something for my dad."

"GW Antiques and Curiosities? Seriously? That's where you want to shop for your dad?" says Becca. "I'm not going in. Those places make me nervous."

"I know what you mean," Leigh Ann says. "I'm always afraid I'm going to knock over a stack of china plates that's worth a fortune."

I ignore their fears and run across the street, where I press my face against the front window and peek at the treasures inside. "Come on, you guys. It's not that crowded, and there's some cool old boat models and stuff."

As I step inside, I'm greeted by a woman who is

probably in her thirties, but dressed like she's younger. Her hair is pulled back in a ponytail, and she's rocking a natural, almost-no-makeup look.

"Good morning, er, afternoon," she says, her eyes landing on the rock-star-cool jacket my parents surprised me with a few weeks back. "Wow. That is a great jacket."

She's right about that; it *is* pretty terrific. It's not really warm enough for mid-December, but I just can't bear to put it away until spring. If I have to suffer a little bit to look fashionable, so be it.

"Oh, thanks," I say. "It's my favorite."

The door opens and Margaret comes inside; a few seconds later, Leigh Ann and Becca follow reluctantly.

"Are you all together?" the woman asks. "Of course you are. I'm Lindsay. Is there anything in particular I can help you with today? Or are you just browsing— which is fine, too."

"I'm, um, kind of looking for a present for my dad," I say, eyeing an old wooden model boat hanging from the ceiling above me. "Wow. That is beautiful. He would love that."

"You have good taste," says Lindsay. "That's a Hacker model from 1935, with the original paint. It's twelve hundred dollars."

I hear Becca snickering behind me. "For twelve hundred bucks, I want a boat big enough to ride in, at least."

"That's a bit more than I want to spend," I say. "Maybe I'll look around a little."

I wander over to a display case containing an assortment of items: cuff links of every shape and size, a couple of gold pocket watches, wicked-looking straight razors, engraved cigarette lighters, money clips, and much more. And then I see the perfect gift for my dad.

"Margaret, come here," I whisper. "Do you see it?"

She leans over the case, her eyes scanning the contents until they land on an antique fountain pen. She grins at me. "You're right. It's perfect. Can you see the price?"

"Do you see something you like?" Lindsay asks, moving behind the case. When she realizes which case we're looking in, her face falls. "Oh, this case is . . . special. These are things from the estate of a gentleman who lived in the neighborhood, a Mr. Dedmann. Unfortunately, they're not for sale—not in the usual way, that is. They're all going to an auction next Tuesday evening. Which piece are you interested in, one of the Cartier watches?"

"No, the fountain pen," I say. "Can I see it?"

Lindsay unlocks the case and sets the pen on a felt pad on top of the glass. As I lift it, I smile at the heft of the thing: it is about as far from the cheap disposable pens I use as you can get. The rounded barrel is polished black, sleek and smooth, and the gold nib still looks new.

"It's a beauty," says Lindsay. "An old Reviens— made in France in the twenties. They've been out of business for years."

17

"How much is it worth?" I ask.

Lindsay smiles. "Well, that depends. If it were for sale here in the shop, Mr. W.—he's the owner, I just work for him—would probably ask two hundred dollars for it. But . . . if you were to buy it at the auction, you might get it for a lot less. Depends on who else wants it. And how badly, I suppose."

"Like, how much less?" I ask.

"With something like this, the auctioneer will probably start the bidding at twenty-five dollars. After that . . ."

Margaret and I share one of our are-you-thinking-what-I'm-thinking? looks and grin at each other.

"So, tell us more about this auction."

Chapter 2

A piece of my world crumbles

Mr. Eliot's latest harebrained scheme to torture his honors students is to force us to perform in a one-act Christmas play that he wrote just for us. ("My, aren't we lucky," Livvy Klack, my enemy-turned-friend observed.) It's called *The Merry Gentlemen,* and it is, according to Mr. Eliot, an homage to his hero, Charles Dickens. It tells the story of the two men who come into Scrooge's offices on Christmas Eve, asking for money for the poor. Grumpy old Scrooge, if you remember, runs them out the door, telling them that it's not his problem that people are suffering. A real prince, old Ebenezer.

Mr. Eliot's script picks up from Scrooge's last "Bah! Humbug!" and follows the two "portly gentlemen" throughout the remainder of Christmas Eve, revealing twists and turns in their lives that I doubt Mr. Dickens ever considered. I don't want to give away the whole story, but I can reveal that after their unpleasant experience with Scrooge, the two gentlemen begin to have serious doubts about what they're trying to achieve. In fact, after a few glasses of Christmas cheer, they're so filled with despair that they convince themselves that their mission is absolutely pointless.

We've only been rehearsing for a few days, and Mr. Eliot is driving us crazy by constantly changing our lines. Even Leigh Ann, who is practically a professional actress, is losing her cool. With the help of some oversize thrift-store clothes and a ton of stuffing, she and Livvy are playing the portly gentlemen. They both had almost all their lines memorized when Mr. Eliot broke the news that he was still rewriting some of their scenes.

"Can you do that?" Livvy asks.

"I'm the director and the playwright. I can do anything," he says. "That's why it's so good to be king."

Leigh Ann grumbles under her breath, "Yeah, and that's why there are revolutions."

Our day doesn't get any better after that. As we gather our books and coats from our lockers, I persuade Livvy to join us at Perkatory, our local coffee shop / hangout, for a little unwinding and director-bashing. I lead the way from the school, past the church, and down the steps to the front door, where I stop, my red Chuck Taylors suddenly glued to the concrete. Becca, who isn't paying attention, runs into me, smashing my face right into the door.

"Owww! Ow, ow, ow!" I shriek. "My nose!" My

lovely Gallic nose (inherited from Dad) is still healing from a little run-in it had with Livvy's fist during swim practice a few weeks ago. That whole Mistaken Masterpiece extravaganza may have had a happy ending, with Livvy and me walking down the red carpet to the premiere of Nate Etan's (astonishingly bad) movie together, but my nose hasn't quite gotten over it yet.

"Sorry!" Becca says, unable to suppress a smile.

Livvy cringes with embarrassment. "Oh, man. I am so sorry, Sophie. Are you okay?"

"It's her fault for just stopping like that," says Becca. "What is the matter with you, anyway?"

"Me? How did this get to be my fault? Look at the sign!" I step aside so everyone else can see what has stopped me cold:

CLOSED UNTIL FURTHER NOTICE

"What? That can't be right," says Leigh Ann.

"They can't do this!" shouts an indignant Becca. "It's not fair. What are we supposed to do?"

Even Margaret, usually unflappable, is shaken. "No. Not Perkatory. We need this place. Even with its smelly old couches and the occasional cockroach. It's ours. We have to do something."

She's right. It's not just a coffee shop—it's part of our history. The countless cups of coffee and hot chocolate, the stale pastries, the conversations, Jaz stealing the violin, the music . . . Oh no! The music!

"The Blazers!" I scream. "Where are we going to play?"

The Blazers, in case you haven't heard of us, is our band, and we've had a regular Friday-night gig at Perkatory for the past couple of months. Okay, to be completely honest, it's the only place we've ever played, other than Elizabeth Harriman's basement. We don't actually get paid, but Aldo, the manager, gives us free ice cream every Friday. There's me on guitar, Becca on bass, Leigh Ann on vocals, and our friend Mbingu, the only non–St. Veronica's member, on drums.

Becca groans. "Finished up at the age of twelve. Life is so cruel."

"I'll find you guys another job," promises Margaret, our manager. "But in the meantime, we have to get to the bottom of this. I know just where to go. If it happened in this neighborhood, Malcolm Chance is the man to talk to." She spins around and stomps up the steps.

As we rush off to see Malcolm, I almost knock over a guy who is standing on the sidewalk handing out flyers. He shovels one into my hand as I'm apologizing.

"Half-price coupon," he says in a heavily accented voice. "Grand-opening special."

I'm about to say "No thanks" and hand it back to him (in the interest of saving a tree, or at least a small branch) when "New Coffee Shop" near the top catches my eye.

"Wait!" I shout as my friends swing past me and turn

the corner onto Lexington. I spin back around to the guy with the flyers. "Where is this? *Dónde?*"

To my horror, he points to a building directly across Sixty-Sixth Street, almost a mirror image of the building that is home to Perkatory and our old friend Mr. Chernofsky's violin shop. The awning that extends over the stairs to the lower level is *brand*-new, I realize, and in one of those playful fonts reads:

COFFEETERIA

"What's going on?" Livvy asks. "*Now,* why'd you stop?"

I hold the flyer up in front of their faces. "Look across the street—at the awning."

" 'Coffeeteria'? What a stupid name," says Becca.

"I've heard that name before," Margaret says with a worried expression.

Leigh Ann nods. "Yeah, they're popping up all over the place. Everybody says they're great."

"They're not great. They're evil," I say, which is surprising because I hadn't even heard of them until ten seconds ago. "What are they doing here?"

"That must be why Perkatory's closed," Livvy says. "Aldo probably figures he doesn't stand a chance against them."

When the flyer guy sees how interested we all appear to be, he comes over and hands us a few more.

"No! *No más!*" I shout, tearing them into pieces.

He looks at me like I've lost my mind (an altogether reasonable conclusion, some might say), shrugs, and turns away.

"Corporate stooge!" Becca yells.

"Well, now we really have to go see Malcolm," I say. "There must be something we can do to stop this."

"Looks like we might be too late already," says Leigh Ann.

I cross my arms. "I refuse to accept that."

Way back in September, when Elizabeth Harriman sent us off in search of the Ring of Rocamadour, I was certain that her tweed-loving ex-husband, Malcolm Chance, was our nemesis. Boy, was I wrong! (Hardly an isolated event, Becca would be quick to point out.) He turned out to be a huge help along the way in that case, and in the other two big cases we've had since. He's smart, witty, and, as a professor of archaeology, he understands better than most that when you're looking for evidence, sometimes you just have to keep digging. After knowing him for a few months now, the only mystery that still remains about Malcolm is the nature of his relationship with Elizabeth. They seemed to hate each other when we first met them, but ever since we helped Elizabeth and her daughter reconnect, those two appear awfully cozy together.

So it's not surprising when Malcolm opens the bright red door to Elizabeth's townhouse on Sixty-Fifth Street.

His face breaks into a huge smile when he sees us. "Well, if it isn't my favorite crimson-blazer-wearing detectives! Elizabeth! We have visitors!"

I push Livvy toward him. "Hey, Malcolm, you remember Livvy, don't you? She was my doppelgänger when we switched paintings," I say, referring to the case of the Mistaken Masterpiece.

"Of course, of course," he says. "Livvy, welcome! Good to see you again. Please, come in and get warm, everyone."

"We can only stay a minute," I say, after all the hugs and cheek-kissing. "Our teachers are trying to kill us with homework. But this is kind of an emergency."

"My, that sounds dire," says Malcolm. "Sit. Have a cup of tea." As he says the words, the grandfather clock behind him begins to chime.

"It's a sign," Elizabeth says. "Four o'clock. You simply must stay for tea and tell us your troubles. That's what friends do."

We look at one another and then give in to the inevitable, perching in a perfect, red-blazered row on the couch, like birds on a wire.

"What do you know about Perkatory?" Margaret asks Malcolm. "We just came from there, and it's closed."

"And what's worse," I say, "is that there's another

coffee shop opening up across the street. Part of a *chain*."
The way I emphasize that last word, you'd think they
were selling babies inside. "It's called Coffeeteria. Is that
a stupid name or what?"

Margaret pats me on the arm. "Easy, Soph. Deep
breaths."

I lean back on the couch, following her advice.

"Anyway," Margaret continues, "we figured that
since you seem to know just about everything that goes
on in this neighborhood, you'd probably be able to give
us the real scoop."

Malcolm frowns. "Sorry to disappoint you girls, but
this is the first I've heard of it. Is there a sign, or a notice
from the health department, anything like that?"

"Just a sign saying CLOSED UNTIL FURTHER NOTICE,"
says Leigh Ann.

"I saw the manager—what's his name, Aldo?—last
Thursday," Malcolm notes. "He was outside sweeping
the steps, talking with Ben, from the violin shop. He
waved and said hello; I didn't notice anything unusual.
He was smiling. It's probably nothing."

"We saw him Friday," I say. "We played there on
Friday night, for cryin' out loud. He never said anything
about closing."

"You mentioned something about the health department," says Margaret. "Why would they care about a
little place like Perkatory? It's not really a restaurant;
they just sell a few things to eat."

26

"They still have to pass the inspections. But if that was the problem, there would be a sign saying so. I'll tell you what—I'll look into it for you. The building is owned by someone in the parish. I'll give him a call. How's that sound?"

"Thanks, Malcolm," Margaret says. "You're the best."

"Let's not get carried away," teases Elizabeth. "We don't want it to go to his head. He's hard enough to be around as it is."

"Oh, I almost forgot!" I say, leaping to my feet. "Do you guys know anything about auctions?"

"Auctions?" Malcolm says, grinning ear to ear. "Ladies, when it comes to auctions, Elizabeth here is a true master, an ace, a . . . virtuoso. Auctioneers are mere putty in her hands. They may think that they are in charge—"

"Enough!" cries Elizabeth. "I think they get the picture. He's right, though, girls. I have been known to attend an auction or two." She points at the artwork hanging around the room, paintings by people like Matisse and Warhol. "All from auctions. Every piece. Why do you ask?"

"Well, I found this fountain pen that I really want to buy for my dad for Christmas because it is old, and French, and just so perfect, but then the woman in this shop told me that she couldn't sell it to me because it's already scheduled to be in some auction, and she said that the bidding will start at only twenty-five dollars, but I can even go a little higher because I still have all that money I earned from dog-sitting for Nate Etan, but, oh no, it's tomorrow night!"

"Breathe, Sophie!" Margaret says before taking over for me. "The other problem is that we're too young to bid. You have to be eighteen."

Elizabeth opens her desk calendar and leafs through the pages. "Tomorrow night, you say? Which house? Sotheby's? Christie's?"

"Um, I think she said Bartleman's. Up on Ninety-First. We found the pen in this little shop on Eighty-First, GW Antiques."

"And Curiosities," Becca adds. "You can't forget those."

Elizabeth is already punching numbers into her phone. "Good afternoon. This is Elizabeth Harriman. Can you tell me what time tomorrow's auction begins? Seven-thirty? Lovely. And will the items be available for preview beforehand? Perfect. Thank you very much, young man." She sets the phone on the coffee table and looks at me with a satisfied smile on her face. "It's all set. I'll meet you at Bartleman's at seven o'clock."

"You know their phone number by heart?" Leigh Ann asks.

Malcolm takes a big bite of cookie and winks at Leigh Ann. "Don't say I didn't warn you."

28

Chapter 3

That old pen is chock-full of surprises

On Tuesday at seven o'clock, Elizabeth and Malcolm are waiting for us at the entrance to Bartleman's Auction House on Ninety-First, between Lexington and Third. A sign outside announces the evening's big event: an auction of "some personal effects" from the estate of Curtis Dedmann. Dad is at the restaurant, so Mom joins Margaret and me for this glimpse into an unfamiliar (and, at least to me, kind of creepy) world where people line up to fight over some dead guy's stuff. (Of course, now that I'm one of those people, I guess I really shouldn't judge.) I told Mom about the pen, and she even offered to help me pay for it, as long as the price stays in the "reasonable" range.

Most of my dog-sitting money went into my college savings account, but Mom and Dad let me keep out some for Christmas, as long as I promised not to spend too much on them. When I see the crowd that has gathered inside the showroom at Bartleman's, my heart sinks an inch or two. Surely I'm not the only one interested in that Reviens fountain pen. I cross my fingers as we go inside.

We aren't in the door for five seconds before one of the Bartleman-ites (Bartlemanians?) is fawning all over Elizabeth, giving her the full celebrity treatment. He hands her a catalog and then offers to take her coat, get her a drink, arrange a private viewing of the most desirable pieces, whatever she wants. No kidding, I think the guy would shine Malcolm's shoes if he asked (and if I know Malcolm, he might).

Elizabeth just shakes her head. "Not today, Raoul. I'm here for a friend, and she has her eye on one small item. Here it is—lot number nine, the Reviens fountain pen. Hmmm. I see that it 'appears to be in working order.' Does that mean no one has actually tested it to make certain? That seems odd. I would hate to have my very good friend spend her hard-earned money on a defective pen."

Poor Raoul apologizes like mad and says that he'll see what he can do. I watch as he has a brief, intense conversation with a twenty-something woman with vivid red hair, and then the two of them take the pen from its display case and head into the back room.

Two minutes later, Raoul sets a notepad on an antique desktop and hands Elizabeth the pen. She turns it over in her hands, admiring it, and then signs her name on the pad.

"Ah, lovely," she says. "Sophie, would you like to give it a try?"

"Umm, sure." I've never written with a fountain pen, and I'm amazed at how effortlessly it glides across the page. I find myself writing in cursive for the first time in months; I'd almost forgotten that I knew how!

"Wow! Margaret, you have to try this! I feel like I could just write and write, without my hand ever getting tired."

Elizabeth smiles and thanks Raoul, who looks relieved as he returns the pen to the display. Malcolm, meanwhile, comes back carrying a Ping-Pong paddle with the number eighty-one on it.

"What is that?" I ask.

"Well, I hope it is your lucky number," he says, handing it to me. "You just sit next to Elizabeth, and hold that up when she tells you."

"But only when she tells you," adds Mom. "I don't want you accidentally buying a van Gogh."

"Excellent advice," Malcolm agrees. "Now, if you ladies will excuse me, there are some books I may be interested in. Lot 113, if you're keeping score, my dear. Save me a seat!"

"We have a few minutes before we need to go into the auction room," Elizabeth says, "so feel free to wander around, girls. You might see something else you like—maybe for your lovely mother, Sophie. Perhaps a nice brooch? I see that there are several in the catalog."

"No, no, no," Mom insists. "Don't you dare buy me a thing."

Margaret and I wander off to check the bookcases for possible Mr. Eliot gifts. As we're standing there browsing, out of the corner of my eye I see someone leaning against the glass display case, talking to Raoul. My heart drops into my shoes when I realize that it's Marcus Klinger—the rude guy from the bookstore—and he has my dad's pen in his grubby little hands!

I elbow Margaret. "Oh no. No. No. No."

"What are you . . . ? Oh, him. What is he doing here?" She scowls at him, a reminder that one insults Margaret Wrobel at one's own peril. Something tells me that Marcus Klinger is going to pay dearly for that "clean hands" remark.

Klinger sets the pen on a square of black velvet and examines it with a magnifying glass. He then starts to unscrew the barrel, but Margaret interrupts him, snatching the pen out of his grasp.

"Excuse me, miss, I was looking at that," he says. Then he recognizes her from the store. "Oh. You."

"Yeah. Me. I would have thought you'd be looking at the books," she says. "I'm sure there are plenty of cheap imitations that you could pawn off as first editions in your shop."

Fortunately, Raoul steps in before Klinger challenges Margaret to a duel, or whatever it is that people do now when they think they've been insulted. "Sorry, miss. I must return the pen to the case. It's time to move every-thing into the auction room."

Margaret hands him the pen and then glares one last time at Klinger before joining me back at the books.

"What are you doing?" I demand. "Are you crazy? Now he's going to buy the pen just for spite."

"Don't worry, Soph. Elizabeth knows what she's doing."

"Yeah, maybe. But it's still my money, remember."

The woman with the dazzling red hair approaches, smiling warmly. "Hi, I'm Shelley Gallivan. I'm sorry to interrupt, but I couldn't help noticing your St. Veronica's blazers—that's my alma mater. I have such fond memo-ries of that place. Is Sister Bernadette still the principal? She runs a tight ship, I think you could say."

"Yep, she's still the captain," I say. "I'm Sophie."

Margaret introduces herself, and then asks, "Do you work here?"

"No, I'm just . . . coordinating, I suppose is the right word. I worked for Mr. Dedmann before he died, and now I'm helping out with the settling of his estate. So-phie, I see that you're interested in his old fountain pen. Is it for yourself?"

"No, it's for my dad, for Christmas. He collects them."

"Do you know anything else about it?" Margaret asks.

"Only that it was Mr. Dedmann's favorite," Shelley

replies. "Maybe I shouldn't tell you this, but he was holding it when he died. I found him at his desk, and the pen was still in his hand."

Hmmmm. I'm not quite sure how I feel about that.

"Really?" Margaret asks. "That's amazing. What was the last word he wrote?"

Shelley ponders the question for a second. "I'll have to . . . Oh yes, now I remember. He had the pen in his right hand and an odd metal box in his left—and the last words he wrote were 'Look inside.' He wrote it on the cover of a notebook, almost like he knew he didn't have time to open it to a blank page. The box he was holding is a funny little thing—it has a tricky latch that took me a while to figure out. When I finally did, the only thing inside was a photograph of a young woman. I had to use tweezers to remove it. It was an old picture; based on the hairstyle and clothes, I'd guess it was taken in the thirties or forties. Nothing written on the back except for the letter 'V.' It's still at the house; I'm trying to piece together some of the details of his life. He was a very secretive person, and so much of his life is a complete mystery. Well, I need to get ready for the big auction. It was nice meeting you, and good luck! Hope you get the pen!"

As she scurries off to the back room, Margaret and I join Mom and Elizabeth, who are waiting for us at the entrance to the auction room, where a hundred or so folding chairs are set up.

As Elizabeth leads us down the aisle, I see yet another familiar face in the gathering crowd, although the woman in question is doing all she can to avoid being recognized. But I'm certain it's Lindsay, the woman from GW Antiques, sitting in the last seat in the last row of chairs, a scarf wrapped around her head in that sixties, going-out-for-a-spin-in-my-convertible way. She doesn't see me, or if she does, makes no attempt to smile or wave; she just stares ahead.

We take seats in the fifth row; I'm on the aisle with Elizabeth next to me. My right hand has a death grip on the paddle, while my left presses it against my lap. (Why, you ask? Because I can't trust my right arm not to do something crazy.) Marcus Klinger strolls past, so close that his coat brushes my arm, and takes the aisle seat three rows in front of me.

Margaret leans forward to get my attention. "Go get him, Sophie. That pen is yours."

The auctioneer steps up to the podium and, after all the introductions and warnings, bangs his gavel on the podium to begin.

The first six items are boxes of miscellaneous old books, and Marcus Klinger wins the bidding on every one. The lady who is bidding against him takes her time when the asking price goes above a hundred dollars, but Klinger never hesitates to raise the bid. It's pretty obvious that he wants those books, and is going to pay whatever it takes to get them. Margaret shakes her head every time the auctioneer shouts, "Sold! To number thirteen, in the second row!"

Items seven and eight are sets of bookends: hunting dogs in the first, and owls in the second. Elizabeth takes the paddle from my hand and bids on the dogs, but sets the paddle back on my lap when the price goes to two hundred.

"I can buy them in a shop for that," she whispers to me.

"As if you would pay retail," says Malcolm.

Elizabeth grasps my hand. "Are you ready?"

I nod, gripping the paddle tightly.

"Lot number nine!" announces the auctioneer. "A fountain pen by Reviens. French, circa 1920. Can I have fifty dollars to start?"

Fifty dollars! My head, ready to explode, spins to face Elizabeth, whose eyes quickly scan the crowd for interest at that price. Ahead of me, I see Marcus Klinger sitting at attention, waiting.

"Twenty-five, then," says the auctioneer after an eternity.

Elizabeth nudges me. "Now."

My hand shoots up.

"I have twenty-five, the young lady on the aisle. Can I have thirty? Thirty dollars for this beautiful, working fountain pen."

Grrr. Shut up, mister.

Klinger—grrrr again—raises his paddle nonchalantly.

"I have thirty from lucky number thirteen. Do I hear thirty-five?"

Help! What do I do? I'm starting to panic as I turn to the support team on my right.

Mom nods.

Malcolm gives me the thumbs-up and a wink.

Elizabeth pats me on the arm.

And Margaret just grins like mad. The girl loves to see me squirm.

I raise the paddle, which suddenly feels much heavier in my hand.

"Thirty-five! Do I hear forty? Forty dollars for this excellent example of French craftsmanship. A steal!"

I glare at the auctioneer, gritting my teeth and attempting mental telepathy: Will you please just SHUT UP!

A century passes. My eyes are glued to the back of Klinger's head, and I almost pass out when his shoulder twitches. But his paddle stays on his lap where it belongs, and the next thing I know, the auctioneer shouts, "SOLD! To the young lady with paddle number eighty-one!"

I did it!

"Well done," Elizabeth praises. "That was perfect. Like an old pro."

I catch Marcus Klinger sneaking a peek over his shoulder at our little celebration, a snide expression on his face. A few minutes later, the auctioneer announces lot number thirteen, a walking stick with a sterling silver handle made to look like a sawed-off tree branch.

Malcolm, who sometimes carries a walking stick (not because he needs it—he freely admits that he just likes the way it looks with his tweeds), perks up.

"May I borrow that paddle for a moment, dear?" he asks.

Elizabeth groans. "Another stick? Good grief. There's hardly room in the umbrella stand as it is."

"Yes, dear," says Malcolm with another wink in my direction.

Bidding on that silly walking stick turns into a small-scale war between Malcolm, a man in the back (old and feeble enough that he actually needs the darn thing), and—big surprise—Marcus Klinger. The bidding quickly goes from one hundred, to two, to three, to four. Malcolm's final bid is four hundred fifty, and when Klinger promptly raises it to five hundred, Malcolm mutters, "Too rich for my blood," and hands the paddle back to me.

I'm rooting for the old man, but Klinger keeps raising and raising the bid, never hesitating to hoist his paddle high in the air. Finally, with the bidding at nine hundred dollars, the old man in the back gives up, and Klinger adds the walking stick to his haul, which includes six boxes of books and a small writing desk.

But there's one thing he doesn't have: Dad's fountain pen.

• • •

"Don't you just love New York during the holidays?" Mom says, slipping her arm through mine as we stroll through the pine forests of the Upper East Side on the way home from Bartleman's. "The lights, the smells . . . so lovely. Maybe it's my imagination, but people even seem nicer."

"Well, I'm with you about the lights and the smells, but that other thing is definitely your imagination," I say, picturing Marcus Klinger and the way he treated us in his shop.

Mom squeezes my arm. "Since when did my baby get to be so cynical? What happened to my innocent little Sophie?"

"She started seventh grade," I say. "It's a jungle out there, Mom."

"Don't let a few Scrooges ruin your holidays," Mom says. "You have such a wonderful outlook on life; it's just one big adventure after another for you, and I love that about you. I couldn't bear to watch it disappear. Promise that you won't ever stop being so excited, so *passionate,* about . . . everything?"

"Promise."

When we get home, it's after nine o'clock, and Dad is waiting for us—an unplanned-for scenario. He's usually at the restaurant until eleven or twelve on Tuesdays.

"Guy! What are you doing home already?" Mom asks, caught completely off guard. She recovers quickly, though; Mom is pretty fast on her feet. "I'm sorry—that sounded like we're not happy to see you."

Dad smiles and hugs her. "Nice to see you two, too."

"Two too," I repeat, in a singsongy voice. "Like a train. Get it? Choo-choo?"

Dad stares blankly at me, then turns to Mom for an explanation of my lame attempt at humor.

"Never mind," she says. "Your daughter's being silly. We've been out doing a little Christmas shopping."

"For youuuuuu," I add.

"Ah, *ma foi*! All is forgiven. Was it a . . . successful trip?"

"Very," says Mom. "I think you'll be pleased. Definitely surprised."

"I can't wait to see your face," I say. "I don't know how I'm going to make it to Christmas."

Dad shrugs. "You could just give it to me now if it will make life easier for you."

"Oh, no you don't," says Mom. "Sophie—to bed! Look at the time. And you have a math test tomorrow!"

"Postponed until Thursday," I say. "But I do have a Spanish quiz. No problemo."

I kiss them both and then head off to my room, where I spend a few minutes reviewing my Spanish notes. Before long, I convince myself that I'm fully prepared for the quiz, set my notebook aside, and take the fountain pen out of my jacket pocket. As I unscrew the cap, I realize that I have no idea how the thing works.

I vaguely remember seeing Dad fill one of his other pens: he dipped the end of the pen into a bottle of ink, and somehow the pen sucked up enough ink to write for a few days.

It could use a thorough cleaning, I decide. There is dried ink all over the gold nib, and the silver trim pieces could use a good polishing. I gently unscrew the barrel and start to wipe the inside with a cotton swab, but then something strange happens. The swab catches on something, and as I pull it out, a rolled-up piece of paper comes with it. At first I think it's just part of the pen, but as I unroll it, my heart starts ka-thumping away; even before I read it, I'm imagining it to be a secret message of galactic importance.

Unrolled on my desk, the paper is about six inches long and two inches wide, and desperate to reroll itself into a tube. Across the top, hand-printed in tiny letters, is a short poem:

> Mighty Hector, Caesar, and he,
> Worthy men of antiquity,
> Are but the first of trios three.

> This sheet, aligned on the page
> That begins the tale of his age,
> Reveals advice that is truly sage.

Below that, twelve rectangular holes have been cut in the paper. All the holes are about one-eighth of an inch wide, but they vary in length, with the longest being about an inch. Their purpose is clear from the poem: place the paper on a certain page of a certain book, and a secret message will appear in the boxes. Of course, finding the right page of the right book is the hard part.

Unless your name happens to be Margaret Wrobel, that is.

I call her immediately and tell her about my discovery.

"I would take a picture of it, but you wouldn't be able to read the poem, anyway—it's way too tiny. I didn't even know it was possible to write that small. What do you think it means?"

"No idea—yet. But the first part of the poem sounds like a riddle; it can't be too hard to figure out who the 'he' is. My question is, why hide a clue about finding advice in a fountain pen? We don't really know anything about the guy who owned the pen, other than the fact that he's dead."

"Um, yeah, thanks for reminding me," I say, a little creeped out.

"Wait—remember what that lady at the auction said? The last thing he wrote was 'Look inside.' What if he meant the pen all along?"

"Oh, right—she just assumed he meant the metal box that was in his other hand."

"Which did have something inside—a woman's picture," Margaret reminds me. "I wonder if the two things are related."

"What about this 'first of trios three' line? What's up with that?"

"You've got me. It's all probably nothing. Don't you have some studying to do?"

"Nope. I'm done. No worries, mate."

"Hmm. We'll see, I guess. Well, I want to go over my notes one more time. I'll stop by in the morning. Regular time?"

"*Perfecto. Buenas noches.*"

So you think you want to be a detective, huh? Let's see if you have what it takes. I'm going to give you a little test, but tell you what, instead of a fill-in-the-blank (don't you just hate those?), I'll start you off with a nice easy multiple-choice question:

Who is the "he" in "Mighty Hector, Caesar, and he"? Which name belongs with the other two?

> a. *Achilles*
> b. *Xerxes*
> c. *Odysseus*
> d. *Alexander the Great*

And no peeking at the next chapter until you know the answer!

Chapter 4

How long do you suppose it takes to dust eighteen miles of bookshelves?

But it is a good half hour ahead of "regular time" that Margaret, who lives in an apartment building exactly eleven minutes from mine, sends me a text message. I'm munching on a piece of cinnamon-and-sugar toast (made with Dad's homemade bread, naturally) when my phone springs to life and this text appears:

> I'm in your lobby, because your
> new doorman won't let me upstairs.
> What is his PROBLEM?

I can't help smiling at the perfectly spelled, perfectly punctuated message—it's so Margaret. Tearing off another bite of toast, I text back:

> Y R U here so early????

Two seconds later, in return, I get: !!!!! That is Margaret's way of saying, "Buzz the doorman and tell him to let me come up."

"Hey, Louie!" I shout into the intercom. "It's Sophie St. Pierre. You see that skinny, goofy-looking kid in the lobby—the one in the bright red blazer? Would you please send her up?"

"Who are you shouting at?" Mom cries, rushing into the kitchen. "I thought the apartment was on fire."

"Oh, just having a little fun with Louie, the temp doorman. Haven't you noticed how loud he talks?"

"Maybe he's hard of hearing, Sophie. I can't believe you're teasing him; you used to be such a nice girl."

"I am nice," I insist. "Wait till you see what I got you for Christmas."

"You're supposed to be saving that money you got from that nutty movie star friend of yours. Twelve hundred dollars for a couple of weeks of dog-sitting. Ludicrous. That's more than I made in five years of babysitting when I was your age. And that was watching children, not a silly dog."

Margaret's knocking saves me (and Nate Etan) from further attacks—or so I think.

"Why were you shouting into the intercom?" Margaret asks. "Jeez! I could hear you out in the lobby! Goofy-looking? Skinny? This is how you describe me to strangers?"

"I was kidding. I knew you'd be able to hear me; that was part of the fun. Sheesh. You two used to have a sense of humor." I plonk myself back into my chair and take a huge bite of toast.

"I think she's ignoring us," Mom says, pouring a glass of orange juice for Margaret.

"That's too bad," says Margaret. "Then I suppose she doesn't want to hear what I learned about that secret message she found."

"Secret message?" Mom asks. "Now what?"

Margaret looks my way. "You didn't tell her?"

I shrug. "Ewastoolay," I say with a mouthful of toast.

Mom raises an eyebrow and looks to Margaret for a translation.

"She says it was too late. Apparently, she was cleaning that fountain pen and found a piece of paper rolled up inside it—there's a poem, and . . . Hey, here's a crazy idea. Why don't you go get the paper, Sophie? Pretty please?"

"Only because I'm curious about what you found out," I grumble, gulping down half a glass of orange juice in one swallow.

Mom moves in close enough to look over my shoulder when I stretch the paper out on the kitchen counter. She squints, trying to read the writing at the top, but quickly gives up.

"My old eyes are no match for that," she says. "And

I don't think my reading glasses would help. What's it say?"

Margaret reads the poem aloud:

> Mighty Hector, Caesar, and he,
> Worthy men of antiquity,
> Are but the first of trios three.
>
> This sheet, aligned on the page
> That begins the tale of his age,
> Reveals advice that is truly sage.

"Just whose pen did you buy?" Mom asks. "Who puts something like that inside their fountain pen? What was his name—Curtis Dedmann?"

Margaret nods. "He lived in a townhouse on Eighty-Second Street. He was kind of a recluse, I think. We don't know much about him. Yet."

Mom holds the paper up to the light. "What are all these holes?"

"It's like a decoder," I say. "You put it over a page in a book, and the words that appear in the boxes spell out a secret message."

"Well, that's very exciting," Mom says. "But . . . why? You know what I mean—why go to all that trouble?"

"A good question," Margaret replies. "Especially if all he's offering is some sage advice."

"Yeah, I was going to ask about that," I say. "What does 'sage' mean, anyway? Isn't that an herb?"

47

"Wise," explains Margaret, a dictionary in a plaid skirt. "Although you're right, it is an herb, too."

"So, what did you figure out?" I ask.

"I know who 'he' is," says Margaret. "It's Hector, Caesar, and . . . Alexander the Great."

(Well? Is that who you picked? Give yourself a gold star if you got it right.)

"You seem awfully sure of yourself," I say.

Margaret shrugs. "It was easy. That line about the 'trios three' gave it away. Three trios equals nine, so I just typed in 'Hector,' 'Caesar,' and the number 'nine,' and up pops something called the Nine Worthies. And when I realized that the first word in the second line is 'worthy,' I knew I was on the right track. Back in the fourteenth century, somebody put together this list of the nine men—"

"No women?" Mom interrupts.

"No, just men. Sorry. They were the nine men who were supposed to represent the ideals of chivalry—you know, courage, honesty, honor, that kind of thing."

"The ability to kill other men," scoffs Mom. "Those three are soldiers. That's what you get when you have men deciding who is 'worthy.' "

"Holy cow, Mom. Why are you so anti-man all of a sudden?"

"The first three are all considered pagans," says Margaret. "The next three are Jewish—they're all from the Old Testament: Joshua, David, and Judas Maccabeus. Not the apostle Judas—he was Iscariot. The last three are Christians: King Arthur, Charlemagne, and Godfrey of Bouillon."

"Okay, I've heard of all of those except the last one," I say. "Godfrey who?"

"First Crusade," answers Margaret, whose brain reminds me of a lobster trap I saw in Maine. Once the facts crawl inside her head, they're stuck there forever. "Anyway, we're looking for a book about Alexander the Great. Or all nine of these 'worthies'; maybe it's in the chapter about him."

"Cool," I say. "When do we start?"

After school, the four of us knock on Elizabeth's door, hoping for an update on the Perkatory situation.

The housekeeper invites us inside, immediately reminding me of our first visit to chez Harriman, and of Winifred "Winnie" Winterbottom. Besides being a so-so housekeeper, Winnie was in cahoots with her sleazy, chain-smoking husband, Gordon, my personal nemesis during the quest for the Ring of Rocamadour. She spied on us and passed the information along to Gordon, who then used it to try to steal the ring from under our noses.

Helen, Elizabeth's new housekeeper, is nothing like Winnie, who was carved from a block of granite: gray, cold, and hard as stone. Rather, Helen is a four-foot-nine bundle of cheerful energy, inviting us in and immediately offering to make a pot of "Flower Power" tea, which she somehow knows is our favorite.

"No thank you," I say. "We just have a couple of quick questions for the professor."

"Uh-oh," Malcolm says, appearing at the kitchen door and wiping his hands on an apron that looks as if it has been used to clean up a major environmental disaster. "Questions for me?"

"Just two," says Margaret. "One, have you made any progress on the Perkatory story, and, two, when you were looking at those boxes of books before the auction last night, did you happen to notice any books about Alexander the Great? Or the Nine Worthies?"

Malcolm chuckles. "The Nine Worthies. I hadn't thought of them in years, but, yes, there was a book—three volumes, in a beautiful slipcase, actually. *Nine Worthy Men,* I think it was called. Why on earth are you interested in those old fossils?"

"Wait! What about Perkatory?" Leigh Ann asks.

"Sorry, nothing yet," says Malcolm. "I'm waiting to hear back from Mr. Varone, the building owner. I'll send you a note the second I hear anything. I promise. Am I to understand that there's been no change—no new signs on the door?"

"You understand correctly, good sir," says Becca. "That place is locked up tighter than Helm's Deep."

"It's so depressing," I say. "I thought I was going to

cry when I walked past this morning. And just seeing that ridiculous COFFEETERIA sign across the street—grrrrr. Makes me want to go over there and pull the stupid thing down."

"Back to the worthies," Margaret says. "Malcolm, the books you saw, were they in one of the boxes that Marcus Klinger bought?"

"Klinger? Yes, I'm pretty sure he bought all the books. And overpaid for them, I'd have to say. He seemed determined to buy them. Same thing with that blasted walking stick. Had to have it, too. Just who is this Marcus Klinger character, anyway?"

"He's a jerk, that's who he is," I say. "He owns this cruddy little used-book store up on Eighty-First."

"My goodness, Sophie," says Malcolm. "You are not having a good week, are you?"

"Tell me about it," I grumble.

Margaret tells him the story of our experience in Sturm & Drang Books, and then I bring him up to date on the paper hidden away in Dad's fountain pen.

"And now we have to go back for more Sturm and Drang," says Margaret.

"What? Why?" cries Leigh Ann.

"Because he has *Nine Worthy Men,*" Margaret says. "We don't have to buy it, we just need to look at it for a minute—if he'll let us."

"Well, this time please make sure your hands are clean," Becca teases.

"Have you tried the library?" Malcolm asks.

Margaret nods. "I checked online. Believe it or not, they don't have it. Maybe they used to have one, but someone lost it, and they couldn't replace it. It's been out of print for a long time."

"Okay, then. How about the Strand?" Malcolm asks. "What do their ads say they have, eighteen miles of books? If they don't have it, I'll eat my hat."

"You'd better be careful, Malcolm," I say. "I think you already owe us one good hat-eating. Those tweed caps of yours must taste really good."

"That's a great idea," Margaret says. "Why don't you come with us?"

Malcolm glances toward the kitchen, shrugs, and pulls his filthy apron over his head. "I was going to bake some bread, but it can wait. And Elizabeth called to say she's going out to dinner with her friend Alessandra, so I'm on my own for dinner, anyway."

On the way to the Strand Book Store at Broadway and Twelfth, we decide to turn the search for *Nine Worthy Men* into a competition, with the losers treating the winners to ice cream. It's Margaret and Malcolm versus Becca, Leigh Ann, and me as we hit the doors running.

There's a good reason Margaret picked Malcolm instead of me to be her teammate: she knows that when I walk into the Strand, I'm like a moth in a room filled with flashing lights, flitting from aisle to aisle and table to table. Self-control? HA! It's a bookstore with eighteen miles of books! Within thirty seconds, I have completely forgotten what I'm looking for. Nine . . . something, I try to remind myself, but, really, who cares, because I just stumbled into a whole section that should be called "Sophie's Choices"—so many books by my favorite authors, mingling with a kajillion others that I simply must have. Right now.

Leigh Ann is about to zoom past me, but she puts on the brakes when she sees me with my nose in an old hardcover. "Did you find it already?" she asks.

"What? Oh, um, no. I was just . . . This is a classic," I say, showing her the cover of Walter Farley's *The Black Stallion*.

"Sophie! Come on!"

"Okay, okay," I say, carefully reshelving the book and running after her.

I make it about thirty feet before I spot something out of the corner of my eye—one of those red notebooks, which I just love. This one is jammed in between a couple of worn copies of *The Catcher in the Rye*. When I'm sure that no one is watching me, I take the notebook from the shelf and glance at the cover. There's a piece of masking tape with "DO YOU DARE?" written across it in black marker.

Do I dare? Well, of course I dare. I flip it open to the

first page, where I find the following message, done in neat cursive:

> I've left some clues for you.
> If you want them, turn the page.
> If you don't, put this book back
> on the shelf, please.

"Sophie!" hisses Leigh Ann, who then drags me away by the arm. "Come on!" She grabs the notebook out of my hand and jams it between the two closest books.

"But that's not where it goes," I protest, returning it to its proper place as Leigh Ann physically pulls me down the aisle toward the nonfiction section.

Ugh. Nonfiction. A strange, alien place, this realm of books about real people. I glance back longingly at the fiction section. "But—"

"No! Stay here, and start looking!" Becca scolds. "Do you even remember what we're looking for?"

"Y-yes. Of course. Nine . . . famous . . . guys."

Becca stares at me, openmouthed. "If we lose, you're buying the ice cream."

"Okay, jeez. I get it. It's *Nine Worthy Men*. And you think it ought to be around here? Where are Margaret and Malcolm?"

"A couple of aisles over," answers Leigh Ann.

"Well, that's probably a good sign," I say, my eyes already scanning the top shelf. The fact is, when I want to find a book—even nonfiction—I have a gift.

And my gift doesn't let me down; less than a minute after I start looking, I spot a copy of *Nine Worthy Men*. It's on the lowest shelf, and I dive to the floor to pull it out.

"Hey—got it," I whisper to my teammates.

They join me on the floor just as I realize there's a problem. "Uh-oh."

"Uh-oh?" they repeat.

"There ought to be three books, but I only see volumes two and three. And Alexander the Great is in volume one."

"Naturally," says Leigh Ann. "Nothing is ever easy. Maybe it's around here somewhere. Maybe somebody took a look at it and put it back in the wrong place."

"Did you guys find it?" Margaret asks, puzzled by the sight of the three of us on the floor.

"Sort of," I admit, handing her volumes two and three. "The set seems to be missing the one we need."

She calls Malcolm over to join the search, but after ten minutes, we still have only six worthy men.

"Now what?" Leigh Ann asks.

"Plan B," says Margaret. "Back to Sturm & Drang." Her face looks like she's sucking on a lemon as she says the name of the store.

Becca pulls Leigh Ann and me close, putting her arms around our shoulders. "Since our team, you know, technically found the book, I think you guys owe us some ice cream."

"Hey, that's right," Leigh Ann agrees.

Margaret starts to protest, but Malcolm the Peacemaker (could he be the Tenth Worthy?) holds up a hand to stop us before we even start arguing.

"Let me settle this the easy way: the ice cream is on me. When we get back uptown, we'll go by Perka— Oh, right. Tell you what. Will you take a rain check for the ice cream? Let me have a day or two to do a little digging."

"Oh, I get it," I say. "Digging. Because you're an archaeologist. Clever."

Leigh Ann, who lives in Queens, and Becca, in Chinatown, head home from the Strand, while Margaret and I take Malcolm's offer of a cab ride home. He gets out at Third and Sixty-Fifth and hands the driver enough money to get us up to our neighborhood, which is very cool, indeed.

We're almost there when I remember the red notebook with the intriguing message back at the Strand. When I tell Margaret about it, I consider asking if she wants to go back for it, but it's getting late and I have a ton of homework. I'm pretty sure it will still be there in a few days, and besides, maybe dealing with only one secret message at a time is a good policy.

Chapter 5

Okay, okay, I admit it—my loyalty to Perkatory might be the teensiest bit irrational

Raf calls at eight o'clock, and I stay on the phone with him for an hour, which is unusual for me: I'm just not a big phone person. But it has been a few days since I've seen him, and you can only convey so much information by texting. You see, ours is a long-distance relationship, New York style: he's an Upper West Sider, and I'm Upper East. It's not just the distance and Central Park that are obstacles, the UWS and the UES are like two different countries, and not necessarily friendly ones at that.

The highlight (if you can call it that) of the conversation is when he tells me that he had crossed the park intending to surprise me after school at Perkatory and found it closed.

"Oh. Yeah, I guess I forgot to tell you about that."

"Are they, like, closed for good?"

"That's what we're trying to find out. Malcolm is checking it out for us. He knows the landlord. So, what did you do after you realized Perk was closed? Why didn't you call me? Not that I was around, anyway. We were downtown, at the Strand, looking for this book about Alexander the Great. It's a long story."

"I was getting ready to, and then my mom called and made me go home. But I checked out that new place, Coffeeteria, before I left. It's really nice. They gave me—"

"NO! No, no, no. You did not go in there. Raf, they're the enemy."

He laughs. That's right: Raf laughs. At me.

"It's not funny," I say.

"I'm sorry," he says, still laughing.

In fact, he's still laughing as I hang up on him.

My phone rings seconds later. I have my finger on the power button, about to turn it off, when I notice that it's Margaret and not Raf.

"Hey, I heard from Malcolm about Perkatory," she says. "You won't believe it. The inspector saw a rat. The health department closed them down on the spot."

"What? They forced them to close because they saw one lousy rat?"

Margaret sighs. Loudly.

"Sophie, I love you. You're my best friend and I would do anything for you. But seriously . . . are you crazy? Of course they got shut down! Do you really want to eat at a place that has rats?"

"There must be an explanation," I say.

"Well, apparently the inspector opened a cupboard in the kitchen and this furry little critter was just sitting there, staring right back at him. They're supposed to have an official, 'CLOSED BY ORDER OF THE HEALTH DE-PARTMENT' sign up on the door, but they're trying to keep it as quiet as possible. Aldo is afraid they're going to lose all their business to that Coffeeteria place."

"Well, they already have their first traitor. Raf went there today. I hung up on him when he told me."

"Don't you think you're being just a tiny bit unrea-sonable? Sophie, it's a coffee shop. It's not the end of the world."

"Maybe not. But in the words of Nathan Hale, 'I have not yet begun to fight!'"

"Um, that was John Paul Jones. Nathan Hale was the 'My only regret is that I have but one life to give for my country' guy."

Grrrrr. "Yeah, well, you know what I mean. It ain't over till it's over."

And frankly, my dear, I don't care who said that.

We have an unexpected early dismissal on Thursday be-cause of a heating (or lack of heating) problem in the school. The temperature outside is in the teens, and snow swirls around our feet as we fight the bitter wind that's raging down Lexington Avenue.

When we get to the subway stop at Sixty-Eighth Street for the trip uptown, I unwrap the scarf from my head and curse myself for stubbornly refusing to wear a hat on the way to school because of a morbid fear of "hat head."

At Seventy-Seventh Street, I rewrap my scarf and follow my much-better-prepared-for-the-weather friends up the stairs and then four blocks into the wind to Eighty-First. It's so cold that the usually hearty Christmas tree sellers are huddled around electric heaters inside their huts, probably wondering why they ever left Quebec. And even though it's barely past noon, the sky is so dark that I'm wondering if there's a solar eclipse I didn't hear about.

We're on our way to see that horrible Marcus Klinger at Sturm & Drang Books, and we're less than thrilled about that destination. In fact, some of us are downright grumpy—definitely the first time I've felt that way about a trip to a bookstore. I can't decide whether to blame Klinger or the fact that I have no feeling in my ears.

"It has to be done," Margaret says. "We know he has a copy of the book, and we know how much he paid for it. We just have to make him a reasonable offer. I looked online at some used-book sites, and nobody has it. The guy I talked to at the New York Public Library told me that because it was an expensive three-volume set that was published during the Depression, there were probably only a few hundred printed. People just weren't buying books. So, Herr Klinger may be our only chance."

"But we don't even know what we're hoping to find," says Becca. "What if, after all this, it's just some stupid saying about saving money?"

"That's a chance I'm willing to take," says Margaret. "Come on, you guys—aren't you just a little curious? A secret decoder hidden away in an old fountain pen?"

"Eh," says Becca, trying (and failing most miserably) to hide her smile.

Margaret smiles back at her. "That's what I thought."

"Before we go into Slurp and Drool, can we stop in the antiques shop?" I ask. "I want to thank that lady for helping me out. I'll just be a second."

Okay, so "a second" turns into an hour. But that's the way things go sometimes.

Lindsay is helping another customer in GW Antiques and Curiosities when we go inside, but she smiles at us and tells us to feel free to look around.

"Now," she says as the door closes behind the customer, "how can I help you girls today?"

"I, um, just wanted to thank you for telling me about the auction. I got that fountain pen for my dad; he's going to love it."

"Excellent!" Lindsay says. "I'm so happy for you. It really is a lovely pen. I hope you didn't have to spend too much."

"No, I got it for thirty-five, plus all those extras. With the buyer's premium and taxes, it ended up being closer to forty-five, but that's okay, because my mom decided to pitch in half the money. You know, I thought I saw you there—I guess it was somebody else."

"Me? No, I was there earlier in the day, but I had

another appointment and missed the actual auction. Must have been my doppelgänger."

Out of the corner of my eye, I see Margaret's right eyebrow arch upward. She, too, was certain that it had been Lindsay in the auction room at Bartleman's.

From the back room, a man's voice—raspy and oddly familiar—shouts, "MISS JONES! Come here!"

She excuses herself, and a quick huddle of the Red Blazer Girls follows.

"I've heard that voice before," I say. It gave me goose bumps all over. And then I put the pieces of the puzzle together. "Holy crud. GW Antiques and Curiosities. 'GW' is Gordon Winterbottom! That was his voice—I'm positive. We have to get out of here. That guy hates us. Especially me."

I start for the door, but Margaret blocks my way. "Relax. He's not going to kill us. He doesn't even know we're here. If he comes out, we say hi and go on our merry way."

"He probably doesn't even remember us," Becca reasons.

"So Gordon Winterbottom has an antiques shop," marvels Leigh Ann. "I guess it fits. I wonder if he buys anything, or just goes around stealing stuff. Hey, Soph, maybe that fountain pen was stolen. Wouldn't that be funny?"

"No! That would not be funny," I say. "That would be horrible. I do not want to give my dad stolen property for Christmas. Besides, we know where it came from—the estate of some dead guy."

"Ol' Gordo still coulda tooken it," says Becca, earning the dreaded stink eye and a whomp on the back of the head from Chief Inspector Wrobel of the NYGP (New York Grammar Police).

Lindsay returns to find us all still in a circle. "So sorry, girls. When the boss calls, I must answer."

"Is your boss . . . by any chance . . . Gordon Winterbottom?" Margaret asks.

The question catches Lindsay by surprise. "Y-yes, he is. Do you know Mr. Winterbottom?"

"Sort of," I admit. "We, um, go to St. Veronica's, down on Sixty-Fifth. He used to be a deacon in the church there. Until a few months ago."

"There was a, um . . . an incident," Margaret says. "You may remember reading in the paper, the story about the Ring of Rocamadour."

"You're those girls!" Lindsay says. "Amazing! What a small world. Gordon only opened the shop here about six weeks ago. Ever since his wife left him—"

Four girls, in perfect harmony: "His wife WHAT?"

"Winnie actually left him?" I ask, lowering my voice back to a whisper.

Lindsay nods. "Poor guy. He's heartbroken. He misses her something terrible. I've never met her, but I hear that she's working at that German restaurant over on Second Avenue—the Heidelberg."

"My dad loves that place," Margaret says. "He says they have the best sausage in town, and he considers himself a true connoisseur of sausage."

"Back up a second," I say. "Gordon Winterbottom is heartbroken? I can't believe the guy even has a heart."

Lindsay can't help smiling—just a little. "He might surprise you. He even quit smoking a couple of weeks ago. Of course, that hasn't exactly helped his temperament, but I think he's trying to win her back by showing how he's changed. And he's determined to make a go of this shop. I teased him the other day that he's working so much that he's turning into Mr. Scrooge . . . which, I'm afraid, makes me Bob Cratchit."

"What did he say?" I ask. "No, wait, let me guess: 'Bah! Humbug!'"

"No, he said that he might as well be Scrooge. He has no one to celebrate Christmas with, anyway."

Well, that shuts me up. In an instant, I feel bad for all the mean things I'd been thinking and saying about ol' Winterbutt. I mean, I know the guy's no saint, but nobody should be alone for the holidays.

"We should get going," Margaret announces. "The snow's really starting to come down."

"Are we still going to Slime and Drool?" I ask.

Lindsay raises an eyebrow. "Slime and Drool?"

Margaret punches me on the arm. "Sturm & Drang." She points at the bookstore across the street.

"Ah," says Lindsay, grinning at me. "It is rather aptly named, isn't it?"

"Yeah. What is that guy's problem?"

"Marcus Klinger?" she says, laughing. "How much time do you have?"

"So it's not just us," says Margaret. "Or him having a bad day?"

"No, and no," Lindsay answers. "He's rude to everyone. It's his nature. I've known him for a few years; he even helped me find this job. We're both members of a little music appreciation club that meets in Mr. Dedmann's townhouse every Wednesday night. There are nine of us: we call ourselves Beethoven's Nine."

"Ah, because Beethoven wrote nine symphonies, right?" Margaret asks.

"Something like that," Lindsay says. "But here's an interesting tidbit about Marcus Klinger: he is a direct descendant of Friedrich Klinger, a German who wrote a play, strangely enough, about the American Revolution called *Sturm und Drang*. Marcus is very proud of that connection. Are you looking for a particular book?"

"Sort of," Becca says. "We started out looking for one thing—a book for our English teacher—but now we're trying to find something called *Nine Worthy Men*. Sophie found—"

Margaret cuts her off. "What do you know about Curtis Dedmann? Who was he?"

My Sherlock-sense detects a momentary narrowing of Lindsay's eyes, as if she's suspicious of our unexpected interest in Dedmann. And suddenly, Madame Zurandot's advice to "trust no one" rings in my ears.

"Curtis was always a bit of a mystery, to tell the truth," says Lindsay. "I knew him for years, but I couldn't tell you much about him. Do you girls live nearby?"

"Sophie and I do," Margaret answers.

"Then you've probably seen him out walking his dog. He had an English setter named Bertie. Beautiful. And you never saw him without his walking stick."

"The one that Marcus Klinger seemed so determined to get his hands on last night, I'll bet," Margaret says softly.

"Hey, I remember that guy!" I say. "When I was taking care of Tillie, we ran into him and his dog a few times. He was nice; he always had a treat for Tillie. She remembered him, too—she used to pull me down the street to see him and get her cookie."

"That was Curtis," says Lindsay. "And now you know almost as much about him as I do."

Hmmm. Somehow, I doubt that.

Chapter 6

No, as a matter of fact, I'm not a member— I can't imagine how they got my number

The bell jangles loudly, announcing our return to Marcus Klinger's bookstore. Margaret insists that we all put on our best chipper and cheerful faces for this necessary-but-unwanted reunion, but Klinger, hidden behind a stack of books, scares the gee willikers out of us when—poof!—he suddenly materializes.

"May I help you?" he asks, almost smiling . . . until he recognizes us. "Oh. You. Again."

Great to see you, too, Klingon.

"I suppose you've come back for the Dickens. Shall I get it down?"

"No, we're looking for something different this time," says Margaret, maintaining her smile. "It's a three-volume set called *Nine Worthy Men*. Do you know it?"

We're all watching his reaction, and we all notice the same thing. His eyes widen momentarily, revealing something. We don't know what that something is yet, but you can bet your faux-fur-lined boots we're going to find out.

"Of course I know it. I wouldn't be much of a book dealer if I didn't." He aims those beady eyes of his directly at Margaret. "Why, in heaven's name, are you looking for that particular book? I thought kids today were only interested in books about vampires. Besides, a complete set is quite valuable—I'd say something on the order of two hundred dollars. Maybe two-fifty in the original slipcase. If I had one, that is. Which I don't."

Bbbrrrinnnggggg! Hello? . . . What's that? You're calling from the New York Chapter of Liars Anonymous? And you want to talk to Marcus Klinger? Uh, yeah. I'm not at all surprised, because, let me tell ya, he just told us a whopper.

Seriously. I'm looking right at the full set of *Nine Worthy Men* (in a slipcase!) locked away in a glass cabinet behind the counter.

I clear my throat, loudly, and point at the cabinet. "Excuse me, Mr. Klingon, er, Klinger, but isn't that exactly what we're looking for?"

He turns his squinty gaze on me. "That's my private copy. It's not for sale. But you didn't answer my question. Why *Nine Worthy Men*? Perhaps I can help you locate another copy."

"We're doing some . . . research," Margaret says. "We're especially interested in the first volume, the one about Julius Caesar, Hector, and Alexander the Great. We don't necessarily want to buy it. If we could just, um, borrow it for a few minutes, I'm sure we could get what we need."

Klinger turns toward the cabinet, and for a second I think he's going to hand it over to us. "I'm afraid not."

"You won't even let us look at it?" Becca asks, indignant. "Why not?"

Klinger half smiles, half sneers (smeers?) at Becca. "It's quite simple, actually. I'm not a fool, girls. Obviously, you discovered something in that old fountain pen, something that, tragically, I overlooked. Whatever it is, it does not concern you, but it is of considerable interest to me. My old friend Curtis Dedmann had a strange sense of humor, you see, and this little treasure hunt was his parting gift to me. You paid what—thirty-five dollars for the pen, plus premiums, no? I will give you one hundred dollars right now for the pen—and whatever you found inside."

"No thank you," I say. "I bought it for my dad, and he is going to love it."

"Five hundred dollars," Klinger blurts out. "Surely with that much money you could find another fountain pen for your father. You could buy ten. I could help you find them."

Now, I don't know much about playing poker, but I know when somebody has shown their cards too soon.

It's pretty obvious that Klinger is desperate to get his paws on that grid, which means that whatever that clue leads to, it must be something special.

"Sorry," I say. "It's my private pen. It's not for sale."

I get a text message from Malcolm the moment we step out of the warm and cozy Sturm & Drang and into the bitter December afternoon.

"Well, that's good timing," I say. "Malcolm found a copy of *Nine Worthy Men* at the Columbia University library; he's on his way to Elizabeth's with it right now."

And so, forty numb toes and eight numb ears later, we arrive at the blazer-red door to Elizabeth's town-house.

When we get inside, we're treated to a most welcome sight, one that is all too rare for New Yorkers: Elizabeth has a roaring fire going in her fireplace! We shed our coats and boots and race to claim the valuable real estate directly in front of the flames.

"Oh, man, this feels good," says Leigh Ann. "It's just in time, too. It's been an hour since I felt my toes. I'm not even sure they're still attached."

Helen brings us hot chocolate with marshmallows, and by the time Malcolm arrives, the blood is moving through our extremities.

"Hail the conquering hero," he shouts, waving the book over his head.

"Yippee," offers Elizabeth sarcastically. "Now tell

the girls what you told me. It was your assistant who found the book, not you."

"A technicality," replies Malcolm. "It was my expedition; therefore, I get the credit. That's the way it works in archaeology."

He hands the volume to Margaret, who flips through the pages until she finds the start of the section devoted to Alexander the Great.

"Okay, Sophie. Break out the grid," she says.

Each page of the book is printed with tiny type, in two columns, which, according to Malcolm, was common during the Depression and World War II, as a way to conserve paper. The grid that I discovered inside the pen is exactly the length and width of one of the columns, and I set it down on the left-hand column, quoting from the poem printed at the top. "Aligned on the page . . . that begins the tale of his age."

Through the twelve rectangular holes, this is what we see:

pull
the
ribbon
and
You'll
see
the
walking
stick

is

the key

Together, we read the words aloud: "Pull the ribbon and you'll see the walking stick is the key."

"Pull what ribbon?" Becca asks.

"The key to what?" wonders Leigh Ann.

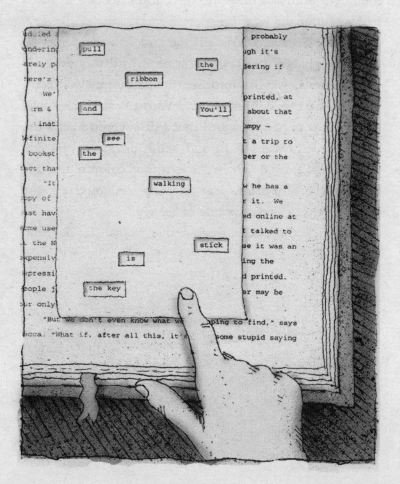

Malcolm takes the book in his hands and shows us the attached ribbon bookmark, which had been tucked between pages in the section on Julius Caesar. "You used to see these in a lot of books. Not so much anymore."

"My mom has a cookbook with one like that," says Leigh Ann. "Do you think that's the ribbon we're supposed to pull?"

"Worth a try," says Malcolm, tugging gently.

"What if it's, you know, like a trigger?" I ask, leaning away from him and waiting for the big explosion.

But this ribbon isn't budging. Malcolm takes a closer look and declares it to be untampered with; it is still solidly glued into the binding of the book. "If I pull any harder, I'm just going to rip it out."

"Well, that settles it. We need Dedmann's copy," says Margaret. "He left a message in his pen, about pulling a ribbon in a book that he has in his library. But now Marcus Klinger has it."

"And he is never going to let us see it," I say. "And even if he did, he's certainly not going to let us yank the ribbon out of it."

Malcolm shakes his head angrily. "The walking stick! I knew I should have kept bidding. It's the key . . . to something."

"Um, guys, I'm really confused," Leigh Ann says. "Have I missed something, or do we still not know what we—or this Klinger guy—are even looking for? I mean,

I understand about the book and the ribbon, but then what? What is, you know, at the end of the rainbow?"

Everyone turns to Margaret for an answer, which she (of course!) provides.

"We don't know, but it must be something really valuable; look at what Klinger is going through to get it for himself. I don't know about you, but I kind of get the feeling that Lindsay, the woman from the antiques store, knows a lot more than she's letting on. I think we have to pick her brains."

Before I can beg Margaret not to make me go back out into the cold, Becca jumps to her feet. "Malcolm! Elizabeth! You are not going to believe what else we found out today! The Winterbottoms! They split up!"

Elizabeth comes running from the kitchen. "What! Gordon and Winnie? Wherever did you hear that?"

"Remember the shop where Sophie found the fountain pen?" says Becca. "It's called GW Antiques and Curiosities. The 'GW' stands for Gordon Winterbottom. He just opened it a few weeks ago. Lindsay works for him. She says he's got a broken heart, if you can believe that."

"Did he . . . ? Did you see . . . ?" Malcolm starts to ask.

"No," I say. "He was in the back the whole time."

"Winnie is working at the Heidelberg," Margaret adds. "I actually feel a little sorry for them."

"That makes one of us," I say. "I still haven't forgotten how he tried to frame me for stealing that stuff from the church."

"Maybe he has turned over a new leaf," says Malcolm. "Stranger things have happened."

Chapter 7

Three Wise Men, Christmas Eve, a submarine—
I think you know the rest of the story

Becca and Leigh Ann dig in their (finally warm) heels; no way are they going back uptown to Eighty-First Street.

"Sorry, but I'm going home to my nice warm bed," says Leigh Ann. "And then I'm gonna do . . . nuttin'. I never get to do that. But I have no homework, no rehearsal, no dance class. I'll see you guys tomorrow. You can tell me all about it then."

"And me," says Becca. "You two go right ahead, though. I'm done with antiques shops and old-book stores. I want to see some new stuff for a change."

So it's just Margaret and me who peek in the window of GW Antiques and Curiosities, making sure Lindsay is still working alone before we go inside. She's leaning over a laptop computer behind the counter, reading an online newspaper article with the curious headline "WHERE IS THE THIRD WISE MAN?"

"Remember," I whisper to Margaret as she reaches for the doorknob, "be careful who you trust."

"*Whom*. Got it. But we have to let her think that we trust her. That way she'll trust us."

"How are we going to do that?" I ask.

"I have a plan. Trust me."

"But I'm not supposed to—"

"Sophie."

"Right. I trust you."

"Well, hello again," Lindsay says as we step inside, quickly closing her computer. "But you've lost your two friends. Have you been over at the bookstore all this time?"

"No, we had a little detour, but we had to come back, because we're kind of out of options, and, well, can we trust you?"

Seems like a simple question, right? Lindsay's reaction is interesting, but not simple. She looks surprised, and pleased, and suspicious, all at the same time. (There, I've done it again—created yet another new word: she is surplicious.)

"I—I suppose so, yes. I'm not sure how I can help, but I'm willing to try."

Margaret makes eye contact with me for a split second—long enough for me to understand that it's all part of her plan—and then tells Lindsay an abridged version of my discovery of the grid with the poem and the cutout rectangles, and Marcus Klinger's strange behavior when we asked him about *Nine Worthy Men* (intentionally leaving out the part where Malcolm found us a copy of the book and we were able to use the grid to decode the message).

Lindsay, suddenly eager to leave, glances at her watch. "Oh my. It's later than I thought. Sorry, girls, but I have an appointment . . . across town, and I, um, have to run. Can you give me your email address? Let me see what else I can find out and I'll share it with you."

"That would be great," says Margaret, taking the pen and paper that Lindsay holds out. "So, I guess we'll wait for you to contact us."

"Well," says Margaret when we're a few doors down the street, "I don't know about you, but it seems pretty clear to me. We can't trust her—at all."

"Is that why you gave her a fake email address?" I ask.

She smiles at me. "You see? That's why you're my best friend, Sophie. I knew that you knew it was fake, and for a second I was afraid you were going to say something, but you trusted me. I don't know how this is all going to end up, or how she's involved, but if it's something big, I don't want a bunch of emails from her making it look like we're part of whatever it is that she's up to."

"So, why don't you trust her? I mean, I agree with you, but I'm wondering what it was for you."

"I just don't think she is who she says she is. The way

she slammed her computer shut when we walked in. The way she reacted to everything we said. The way she suddenly had an appointment, it was like she couldn't wait to tell somebody else what we found. And another thing just doesn't quite fit, but I'm not sure what it is. Look how she dresses, her hair, her nails: none of it seems to fit someone working in a funny little antiques shop. Did you notice the article she was reading on her computer—before she closed it?"

"Something about the Three Wise Men, right?"

"The *Third* Wise Man. We need to see what that's all about."

When we get to Margaret's apartment, I shout a hello-I'm-fine-how-are-you-that's-great greeting to her parents and follow Margaret into her room, where I throw myself on her bed and watch her get down to RBGDA business.

She types in the headline, and clicks on the first article that the search turns up. It's from a December 2002 issue of a weekly newspaper from Portland, Maine, and I recognize it at once.

"Hey, that's the one! What's it about?"

Margaret reads for a few seconds. "Wow. I never knew this. This article is about the sixtieth anniversary of something that happened during World War II. In 1942, Nazi spies landed in Maine."

"What, like, in an airplane?" I ask.

"Nope. In a rubber raft. Get this: they were dropped

off from a submarine a few hundred yards offshore, in the middle of a blizzard, on Christmas Eve."

"Wait a second. With World War II going on, a German submarine just parks off the coast of Maine, opens the door, and lets out a bunch of spies, and nobody sees this?"

"It was night, and Maine is a big place, Sophie."

"So, what happened?" I get off the bed to read over her shoulder.

"I'm looking, I'm looking. Okay, well, it appears they made it all the way to New York. They were trying to spy on the scientists who were starting to work on the atomic bomb. They got caught about a month later. Ohhhh. Here's where it gets interesting—*how* they got caught. Back in Maine, some guy reported picking up two men with briefcases in a snowstorm and taking them to the train station. After he dropped them off, he got suspicious, wondering why there were strangers wandering around the middle of Maine in a blizzard on Christmas Eve with briefcases. So he told the police, who told the FBI. When the FBI came to New York, they eventually tracked down the two guys and arrested them.

"But some old lady back in Maine swore that she saw three men walking in the snow that night. Since only two men bought train tickets, and all the other eyewitnesses reported seeing only two men, the FBI basically ignored her. They never officially closed the case, though, because there was one agent—a guy named Vernon Ryerson—who believed there was a third man. Oh, this part is funny: they started calling the phantom spy the Third Wise Man because he came on Christmas Eve and then just disappeared."

"So they never caught him?" I ask.

Margaret scrolls down through the rest of the article. "Sounds like most people don't even believe he existed. But to answer your question, no, they never caught him. They never found another shred of evidence about him. The article from 2002 supposes that if he ever existed, he is long dead and buried." She stops to think about that for a second, calculating the age of somebody who arrived in Maine in 1942. "Maybe, maybe not. If he was in his twenties when he got here, he could still be alive. Of course, he'd be in his nineties."

"I wonder why Lindsay was reading about this. And more importantly, why she didn't want us to see it."

Margaret types in "German submarine Maine spies" and finds several more stories related to the same strange episode. There are some hard-to-read articles scanned from old newspapers, and then updates of the story from the fifties, sixties, and seventies that all focus on the same two questions: One, was there a third man? And, two, if he did exist, what happened to him?

Very good questions indeed.

Big surprise waiting for me when I get home. Correction: Not big. Huge. Sitting across from my mom at the kitchen table is none other than Raf.

"What are you doing here?" I ask.

"Sophie!" says Mom. "That's not very nice. He came here to see you."

"He's a traitor. Coffeeteria! Phooey."

"Maybe I'll give you a few minutes to talk in private. I'll be in my room. Just don't kill each other, okay?"

"When's dinner?" I ask, catching a whiff of Mom's famous meat loaf. "I'm starving."

"It's in the oven; it'll be ready in half an hour. Where have you been, anyway? Leigh Ann called for you a while ago; she said your cell phone must be turned off. I was starting to worry."

"I was with Margaret," I say, revealing no more than necessary. "I have my phone, but the battery's dead."

"Shocking," says Raf, earning him a stuck-out tongue.

Stupid phone. I am constantly forgetting to recharge it, despite the steady stream of troubles that has caused me—a fact that Raf knows all too well. I mean, c'mon, America! We figured out a way to fry Snickers bars and pickles, but we can't make a cell phone battery that lasts more than ten minutes?

I glare at him across the table. "So, what are you doing on this side of town, anyway? On a weeknight?"

"My mom is at a movie on Eighty-Sixth with a couple of her friends. I have to meet her back there in a few minutes. I have something I've been trying to talk to you about, but you haven't been answering my calls—and don't tell me it's because you forgot to charge. You're ignoring me."

And then, just as I'm planning to really let him have it for betraying me and Perkatory, he does something truly, truly awful. He tilts his head just so, causing his hair to fall perfectly across one eye.

Gulp.

Be strong, Sophie. Look away. And for crying out loud, whatever you do, don't look into his eyes!

Too late. He's smiling at me, and my defenses crumble completely at the first sight of his pearly whites, doggone it.

"You are such a jerk," I say, failing miserably in my attempt not to smile back at him.

"I know. But I have some information that you might find interesting. I went back to Coffeeteria—"

"You what! How could you? When?"

"Oh, hold on a second. It was yesterday, when I was hanging out with my uncle after school. He needed something from some plumbing supply store over on this side of town, and it's right down by St. V's. He asked me if I knew anyplace in the neighborhood to get a coffee—what was I supposed to do? We went inside, and while I was ordering our drinks, I saw something really strange. The manager was working at the cash register, and as I'm talking to him, I see these little whiskers popping up out of his coat pocket, followed by a nose and two beady little eyes. The guy just gently pushes the critter back down into his pocket—he doesn't know I saw it."

"He has a pet rat?" I ask. "That's very interesting, because—"

"Because a rat is what got Perkatory shut down," Raf says, finishing my thought exactly. "I overheard some kids talking about it."

"I think I smell a rat," I say. "I knew it! There's a conspiracy to shut down Perkatory to make way for a whole . . . um, cluster of cookie-cutter Coffeeterias. Pretty soon, there'll be one on every corner. Raf, we have to do something."

"Like what?"

"Like clear Perkatory's good name. Who knows how high this goes—the landlord, the health inspector, even the mayor!"

"Do you really think the mayor cares enough about a coffee shop to get involved in this conspiracy? Even one with a cool name like the Cookie-Cutter Coffeeteria Conspiracy."

"Don't be so naive, Raf! This isn't just about Perkatory; it's about the very soul of the city. So, you're going to help me, right?"

As if he has a choice.

When I tell Raf the story about the spies landing in Maine and the FBI manhunt for the Third Wise Man, he says something that gets my attention.

"That sounds a lot like an old movie I saw with my grandfather," he says. "It's called *The House on 92nd Street*."

His grandfather worked as a projectionist at a movie theater in Times Square in the forties and fifties, and is a real movie nut. I swear, he and Raf have watched every black-and-white movie ever made. Okay, maybe not every one, but Raf *has* seen a lot of them, and the kid has a remarkable memory for details about each one.

"Directed by Henry Hathaway. Lloyd Nolan and . . . Gene Lockhart, I think. Not great, but not bad. It was actually filmed at a house on Ninety-Third Street. It was about these German spies who were in New York to steal secrets from the guys who were working on the atomic bomb. It was a true story—they really were in a house on Ninety-Second Street."

See what I mean about the details? He's a freak.

"Wait a second. That's strange. There's a movie about spies in a house on Ninety-Second Street. And Lindsay's reading that article about the Third Wise Man and getting all weird when we told her about what I found in the pen. I wonder if she thinks—"

Raf finishes my thought: "—that the pen guy was some kind of spy?"

"Exactly."

Chapter 8

Minds are boggled, and Margaret gets a new Web address

Friday after school the temperature is all the way back up to the midthirties, and we're standing on the sidewalk in front of the house on Eighty-Second Street—the former home of Curtis Dedmann. I elbow Becca. "Remember what Madame Zurandot said? She saw an old man with a cane, standing in front of a blue door with the number nine. Well, Dedmann was old, he used a cane, his door is blue, and it has a nine on it. Freeeaaaakkkyyyy."

"I see two nines," says Becca, suddenly Miss Literal.

"Maybe Madame Z. couldn't see the other nine because the guy was standing in front of it. And I forgot to tell you the best part. Shelley—the woman who we're going to see—found him dead at his desk . . . with his pen in his hand."

"Shut up!" says Becca. "Now you're messin' with me."

"No, I swear!" I say. "Just like Madame Zurandot said."

Becca grabs me by the shoulders and looks straight into my eyes. "If you're lying, I'm going to pound you, St. Pierre."

"Okay, everybody just calm down," says Commander Wrobel. "And let these red blazers work their magic."

We follow Margaret up the steps (nine of 'em) to the main entrance, where she pushes the doorbell button. A few seconds later, Shelley Gallivan answers the door; she's dressed in jeans and a Vassar sweatshirt, with her abundant, wavy red hair pulled back into a thick knot.

"Hi! It's Shelley, right?" says Margaret in her most cheerful voice. "Remember us?" She pulls me forward so I'm standing right next to her.

"Oh, from the auction the other night," Shelley says. "And you are Margaret and . . . Sophie."

"And Leigh Ann and Rebecca," says Margaret. "We were wondering—if you're not too busy—if we could talk to you about something."

"Why, uh, yes, I suppose so. Come in out of the cold."

Once we're inside, she leads us into a comfortable denlike room with dark paneling and a fireplace, in which there is a barely smoldering fire.

"Are you cold?" she asks. "I can stoke the fire if you'd like."

"No, we're fine," I say. "Boy, this is a great old house. Mr. Dedmann lived here all by himself?"

"I'm afraid so," says Shelley. "It was just him and Bertie, his dog, knocking about this old place. Now, what can I do for you girls?"

"It involves Mr. Dedmann, and his things, and this house," Margaret explains. "There is something going on—something to do with Mr. Dedmann—and, well, right now we're not sure who we can trust. But since you're a St. V's alumna, we figure you can't be all bad."

"Well, you certainly have my attention," Shelley says. "Go on."

"It started the night of the auction," I say, reaching into my backpack for the rolled-up grid. "Remember, you told us that Mr. Dedmann's last words were 'Look inside,' and you found that old picture in the box he was holding. Well, I found this inside the fountain pen."

Shelley carefully unrolls it and reads the poem. She then holds the paper up to the light to examine the twelve rectangular holes. "What is it?"

"It all has to do with a book that Mr. Dedmann used to own, which is now owned by Marcus Klinger—"

At the mere mention of his name, a dark shadow seems to pass across Shelley's face.

"We figured out that the riddle refers to Alexander the Great, one of the Nine Worthies," Leigh Ann says. "And if you set this grid on the page where his story begins, the twelve words that show up are: 'pull the ribbon and you'll see the walking stick is the key.' So, now we know that we need to pull the marker ribbon attached to Mr. Dedmann's own copy of the book, *Nine Worthy Men,* but—"

"Marcus Klinger bought that copy of the book at the auction," Margaret adds.

"And he won't let us touch his copy," Becca finishes.

"There's no chance Mr. Dedmann has another copy lying around here, is there?" I ask.

Shelley shakes her head. "Afraid not. I've been through all the books left in his study, and I'm positive it's not there."

"Do you have any idea what this is all about?" Margaret asks. "Do you know much about . . . Mr. Dedmann's past?"

"To tell you the truth, no, I don't know much about his past; I only knew him the last year of his life. It was kind of strange, to tell the truth. I was finishing up my last semester in grad school when, out of the blue, I got a call from his lawyer, Mr. Garrison Applewood. He told me that Mr. Dedmann wanted to hire me to catalog his music collection—he owns hundreds of original manuscripts from a number of different composers—and maybe even help him write a memoir. It was . . . Well, it was like a dream come true. A job in Manhattan, the chance to work with an amazing collection, and best of all, the position came with a place to live, so I didn't have to go through the usual apartment-hunting nonsense. I live right here, in the garden apartment. It's much nicer than anything I could afford on my own."

"You didn't know him before that?" I ask.

Shelley shakes her head. "I'd never even heard of him. When I asked Mr. Applewood why Mr. Dedmann picked me, he said that one of my professors had recommended me for the job, but I never really believed it. I didn't want to ask too many questions because I was afraid he would change his mind."

"Did he ever say anything about the Nine Worthies?" Margaret asks.

"No, I never heard him mention them, but there is something you should see—in the basement. A room like no other. I think you'll be amazed."

She heads down the first-floor hallway, beckoning us to follow. A spiral staircase takes us a full level below the garden apartment, and into a room that is unlike any other I've ever seen, at least in New York. I have seen rooms like it before, though—in castles in France! First of all, it's enormous: it stretches the length of the entire building, which must be eighty or ninety feet.

And second, it's beautiful, in that dark-and-stormy-night-in-a-castle kind of way. The ceiling, a good twelve feet above our heads, is arched stone, and reminds me of the secret passageways we discovered in St. Veronica's Church. There's one big difference, though: on this ceiling, somebody has painted the solar system and the constellations in incredible detail. The sun, blazing in yellows and oranges that are so bright I swear they're giving off heat, must be six feet across. The planets stretch the length of the room, with sorry-but-you're-not-quite-a-planet-anymore Pluto a dim gray disk in the farthest corner. In the spaces between the planets, gold-leaf stars form the twelve constellations that make up the signs of the zodiac.

"Whoa! That is cool," says Becca, staring up at Jupiter, with its brightly colored bands, distinctive red spot, and multiple moons.

"If you think that's cool, check this out," I say, pointing to the enormous round table in the center of the room. It is surrounded by nine chairs, and like the ceiling, the top has a celestial-themed paint job. A spiraling mass of stars—thousands of them, most in red and blue—cover the surface, glittering under layers and layers of clear varnish.

"That's our galaxy," Margaret informs me. "The Milky Way. Astronomers estimate that it contains more than two hundred billion stars. And it's just one of billions of galaxies. It's mind-boggling."

"Oh, my mind is boggled, all right," I say. "I mean, who needs the Internet when we have you?"

"Yeah," agrees Leigh Ann. "We should just call you Margapedia."

Margaret does her best to ignore us. "This must be where Beethoven's Nine had their meetings. Now that they are Beethoven's Eight, I wonder what they'll do."

"I don't know about that, but check out this floor," says Becca. "I was so busy looking at the ceiling that I almost missed it."

Polished white marble—acres of it—covers the cellar floor, but down the centerline of the room, three large squares of black, each a three-by-three grid of large tiles, are bordered by reddish-brown stone. A brass medallion marks the center of each of the black tiles, and Margaret kneels down to get a closer look.

"The floor is extraordinary, isn't it?" says Shelley.

She stands in the middle of the square closest to the back of the house. "These are the nine Muses of Greek mythology. The other two are the nine planets, and—"

"—the nine worthy men," finishes Margaret, standing on the medallion in the third square. "Here is our old friend, Alexander the Great."

"Boy, this guy has, er, had an issue with the number nine," says Becca.

Shelley smiles. "So you've noticed." She turns and walks toward the back wall, gently touching the wood paneling that stretches from floor to ceiling. She points to the thirty-six smaller medallions (yep, I counted, and, yep, thirty-six is a multiple of nine) centered on the wood panels surrounding us. "These smaller brass medallions represent mankind's highest achievers. According to Mr. Dedmann, they are the top nine in art, music, literature, and science. Here's Galileo, and Goethe, and Wagner, and Rubens. It's fascinating, really. And if you'll pardon the expression, you ain't seen nothin' yet."

Chapter 9

Ironic, don't you think, that this is chapter 9?

Shelley directs us to take seats around the table before she continues. "Mr. Dedmann only brought me down here a few times, but each time, he told me that one day he was going to tell me a secret about this room, and about him—a huge secret, he said. I was dying to know what it was, but I didn't dare press him. Mr. Dedmann could be . . . well, 'difficult' I suppose is the best word. One day he seemed to trust me completely, and then the next he would be very secretive, unwilling to share any information—even details I needed to know about his music collection. I hesitate to say it, but he could be a little . . . paranoid. Whatever his secret was, he was terrified it would be discovered."

"Are you thinking what I'm thinking?" I whisper to Margaret.

"Probably."

Shelley continues: "Then one day we were down here preparing for one of his Beethoven meetings, and he said something about a combination. I asked him if he had a safe in the house, and he just smiled. He walked over to that wall, the one at the back of the house. He placed his hands against it and looked all around the room—at the walls, the floor, the ceiling, everything. Then he looked me right in the eyes and said, 'In this cellar, my dear, are all the answers. You just have to know where to look for the questions.'"

"What do you think he meant?" I ask.

"I'm not sure. Once, out of curiosity, I counted the number of steps it took me to walk from one end of the room to the other, and then did the same thing upstairs. It's the same distance in both directions as the upper floors, which makes sense, right? But then one day I saw something strange. We were down here together, and when we finished what we were doing, he sent me up ahead of him. I started to climb the spiral stairs, and then, I know I shouldn't have done it, but I sneaked back down just far enough to spy on him."

The four of us lean across the table, eyes wide.

"What did you see?" Leigh Ann asks, her voice barely a whisper.

Shelley points at the paneled wall behind me, where Johann Sebastian Bach's medallion is attached. "That wall was opened up like a door, and Mr. Dedmann was inside for a while. It was dark, so I couldn't see what was there, but when he came out, I could see that he was trying to conceal something under his jacket. He pushed the door closed, and that's when I hurried up the stairs. My heart was pounding—I was so afraid he would see me and fire me on the spot."

"Sophie would have tripped and fallen down the stairs," says Becca. "She's the worst snoop ever."

I can't deny that. It's a sad fact that I am the world's most incompetent criminal.

"But it proved something to me. . . . Somehow, the basement is bigger than what's above it," Shelley says.

Margaret is on her feet, completing a thorough examination of Mr. Bach's wood panel. She runs her fingers all around the edges. She taps. She pounds. She presses her ear against it. She sniffs. When she gets to the brass medallion, she looks it over very carefully before touching it. "What are you hiding in there, Johann?"

"I see that you're on a first-name basis with Bach," I note.

Around the outer ring of the medallion, a six-inch circle, is engraved "JOHANN SEBASTIAN BACH, 1685–1750." The center is a sculpture of his face that sticks out a couple of inches. But between the outer ring and the sculpture is a second ring, half an inch wide, with nine stars, each a slightly different shape, cut deeply into it.

As Margaret touches the ring with the stars, she gasps when it moves under her finger. "Did you see that? This part moved." She slowly spins the stars all the way around, clockwise at first, then counterclockwise. "I can feel it . . . clicking inside, like there are gears or something."

Within seconds, we discover that all thirty-six medallions have one movable ring built into the design. The shapes cut into them are different, but each has exactly nine. Nine circles, nine triangles, nine octagons, nine ovals, and so on.

"Again with the number nine," says Becca.

Leigh Ann is on her hands and knees, crawling over the nine planet medallions, stopping on Jupiter. "Hey, these are different! It's the center that moves."

The floor medallions—Nine Worthies, nine planets, and nine Muses—are larger than those on the walls, and are perfectly flat. In place of the sculpture that sticks out on the wall medallions is an elaborate engraving, and in the center of that is an oddly shaped, inch-deep indentation.

Leigh Ann has her fingers in the indentation, trying to move it. "I can't really make it turn, but I can wiggle it a bit," says Leigh Ann. "There's like little . . . buttons down in the hole. Same thing with Mars."

"Wait! Do that again," Margaret says. "Wiggle Mars, just like you were doing before." She puts her ear on the Bach medallion. "When you wiggle it like that, I can hear it in here. It's like they're connected, like they're . . . all . . . part . . . of . . ."

Her voice trails off as she makes the leap to mental

hyperspace, leaving us mere mortals in her wake. Muttering to herself all the while, she scurries from the Muses to the worthies to the planets, lying facedown on the floor to examine each medallion with her magnifying glass. Then she makes a complete circuit of the room, pausing to look at every artist, composer, writer, and scientist, finally coming to stop in front of Mr. Bach.

"Sophie, go to Saturn and kneel down next to the medallion," she says. "Leigh Ann, you go to Hector, and Rebecca, one of the Muses. Good. Now, when I point at you, jiggle the center just like Leigh Ann was doing earlier."

"What's going on?" Becca asks.

"You'll see," says Margaret.

Her smile widens with each wiggle of the brass medallions. "Incredible. Whoever created this was an absolute genius."

"Are you going to share?" I ask.

"The whole thing—the floor, the walls, all these medallions—is a giant lock. It's ingenious. Instead of numbers, the combination is made up of planets, and Muses, and the Nine Worthies."

And then it hits me like a ten-ton sledgehammer (courtesy of the Acme Sledgehammer Company, naturally). "The walking stick is the key!" I shout. Everyone looks at me as if I have flipped. "Don't you see? Remember the clue? I'll bet you anything that the end of the walking stick is shaped just like this"—I point to the indentation in the center of Saturn's medallion—"and when you give it a turn, voilà! The lock opens."

"If you know the combination," says Margaret. "But I think you're right about the walking stick. That would explain why Klinger was so determined to buy it. He must know how this works and is trying to open it."

Shelley's face clouds over suddenly. "Oh no."

"What's the matter?" Leigh Ann asks.

"Mr. Klinger isn't trying to open the lock. He's trying to stop me—or anyone else—from opening it before the end of the year."

"But . . . why?" Margaret asks.

"Because I have to be out of the house by December thirty-first. The only reason I'm still here is the slow pace of lawyers and probate courts. You see, Mr. Dedmann left the house to Mr. Klinger and the rest of the Beethoven people. But all the contents of the house, except for some of the furniture, were left to me. That's why we were able to have the auction that you went to. But once I'm gone . . . I know it's mean to say this, but I don't think Mr. Klinger can be trusted to carry out Curtis's wishes. If he finds anything of value, he's not going to tell anyone. He's been spiteful to me ever since he learned that I was a beneficiary of the will. He even accused me of improperly influencing Mr. Dedmann."

"What a jerk," says Leigh Ann. "Just because you're pretty . . ."

"Why didn't he leave everything to his relatives?" Becca asks. "Isn't that what people usually do?"

"Or perhaps to some other deserving person. Someone like . . . me?" I suggest.

"Yeah, a fifteen-room house is just what you need," Margaret says. "You can't keep one little bedroom clean."

"Neat people are boring," I say.

"Getting back to Rebecca's question," Shelley says, "I'm not sure if he had any relatives. Certainly none that he ever talked about."

"This place must be worth a fortune," Leigh Ann says. "No wonder Klinger wants you out. They're probably going to sell it as soon as they can."

"Well, we need to figure out what's behind these walls," says Margaret. "And that's all there is to it. He said it himself: all the answers are down here in this cellar."

"Oh, I almost forgot," I say. "You said that when Mr. Dedmann came out from behind the wall, he looked like he was carrying something. Did you ever see what it was?"

"Come upstairs with me," Shelley says. She leads us up the spiral stairs to the first floor, and then into the kitchen, where she opens the door to a small under-counter refrigerator and removes an empty wine bottle. "This is where he kept his wine. Now, I can't be sure that this is what he had under his coat, but I don't know where else it could have come from. I did some shopping for him that morning, just as a favor, and also picked up the two bottles of wine he had ordered at a wine shop earlier in the week. When I put them into the cooler, I rearranged all the bottles. And this one was definitely not in there; I would have remembered such an old-looking label. When I saw this in the trash bin, I started to wonder. That's why I kept it."

"What do you think, Sophie?" Margaret asks, handing me the bottle. "You know about wine."

Shelley lifts an eyebrow. "You do? Because I'll confess, I know nothing."

"Well, a little," I admit. "My dad is French, and, well, you know. They're crazy about wine. Let's see, Château Latour, 1949. Wow, that is old. Um, it's from Bordeaux, which is where my dad grew up, and I think I've heard of it. Can I take this to him? He can tell me all about it. Way more than you would ever want to know, even."

"Sure. If you think it might be helpful."

"One more thing," says Margaret. "When we met the first time, you told us about a picture and the notebook he wrote his last words on. Can we see those?"

Shelley retrieves them from the top drawer of a desk in the front hallway and sets them on the counter.

"She's beautiful," I say, holding up the photo of the young woman. "She looks like a movie star. I wonder who she was."

The only clue as to her identity, however, is that single script "V" on the back.

Meanwhile, Margaret studies the notebook. "Look inside," she reads. Flipping through the pages, she lands on one with a list of words and letters that look as if they were scribbled down in a hurry:

WILL TO GA
SI ROTH
SS VOUG
OS FIG

"Have you ever seen this?" she asks Shelley.

Shelley shakes her head. "Never. Doesn't mean anything to me. It can't be that old, though, because I had just bought that notebook for him a few days before he died. Toga? Will? I can't imagine what it's all about. Like I said, Mr. Dedmann had a lot of secrets."

Chapter 10

Velociraptors have nothing on Winifred Winterbottom

As we wave good-bye to Leigh Ann and Becca from the front door of Dedmann's house, it really hits me: it's Friday night, and for the first time in months, the Blazers won't be playing at Perkatory, our regular (and only) gig.

And so, with Dad at the restaurant and Mom playing a concert in midtown, I'm joining the Wrobels for dinner. They don't eat out that often, so I am surprised when Margaret tells me we're going to the Heidelberg.

Surprised and, well, just the teensiest bit terrified. Here's the scene I'm picturing: I'm looking over the menu, trying to decide between bratwurst and weisswurst, when I feel it in my fingertips. At first, it's just a few ripples in my water glass, but when I see the look of terror in Margaret's eyes, I know it's too late. We've been spotted, and Winnie is on the move. Our eyes dart about the room, searching for an escape route, but our attacker is too clever for that; she has made sure that we are seated against the wall, hemmed in by other tables. We are doomed as *Winniesaurus giganticus* moves in for the kill.

Suddenly, Margaret is shouting at me. "Sophie! Are you listening to me?"

The truth is, I have no idea how much of the conversation I've missed. "Huh? What? Yeah. I mean, no. I was having a nightmare."

"Winnie?"

I nod. "What if she's there? She hates us! She used to have a nice cushy job, and now she's on her feet all night serving beer and sausage. What if she's our waitress? She'll probably poison our food! Or, worse, spit in it!"

"That's worse?"

"Uh, yeah. Eeyyukkkk." And then I get an idea. "Margaret, quick, tell your dad I'm allergic to sausage. Tell him I'll die if I'm even in the same room with a dish of sauerkraut."

Margaret, my best friend, the girl I would do anything for, laughs at me. "I thought you liked a little adventure in your life. I seem to remember a motor scooter ride across the park with a certain boy."

"That was different. That was just New York City traffic, and that's nothing compared to Winnie. She's like going up against a herd of tornadoes."

"Well, put on your tornado-fighting shoes, because my parents are waiting for us."

As we approach the Heidelberg, I hang back, letting Mr. and Mrs. Wrobel take the lead. Mr. W. spoils my plan, though, when he holds the door open for me.

"Ladies and guests first," he says, gesturing to me to go inside. I pull my hat down nearly to my eyes, tuck my chin into my scarf, and shuffle through the door.

I shake my head at the hostess, who asks if I want to check my coat. (When the really bad stuff starts goin' down, I want as many layers between me and Winnie as I can get—know what I mean?) My eyes are so busy scanning the room as we move toward our table that I completely miss seeing her come around a corner carrying a tray with four gigantic glass boots filled with beer. (Why boots, you ask? Ummm, I may have to get back to you on that one.) She hoists the tray over my head at the last possible moment, avoiding a catastrophe of epic proportions.

My heart is doing a tumbling routine inside my chest as I drop into my chair.

"Whew! That was close," says Margaret.

"My life flashed before my eyes," I say. "And all I saw was me drowning in a swimming pool full of beer. And Winnie was the lifeguard."

"Shhh!" Margaret hisses. "Here she comes again!"

Winnie, dressed in the traditional German costume, with her . . . um, ample bosom testing the strength of a white cotton blouse, is standing at the end of our table. I slouch down even lower and cover half of my face with my hand as I mumble my order. (I go with the weiss-wurst, by the way. Not traditionally a dinner sausage, I know, but sometimes you just have to be a rebel.)

"Is everything all right, Sophie?" Mrs. Wrobel asks after we've all ordered and Winnie has thundered back to the kitchen (to poison my sausage, I'm convinced).

"Y-yes, everything is fine," I lie.

Winnie returns quickly with our drinks, and this time I see the flash of recognition in her eyes as she sets my soda on the table.

"Miss Sophie, right?" she asks. "From Elizabeth Harriman's place." She turns to Margaret, struggling momentarily to remember her name. "And Miss Marga-ret. I thought you seemed familiar."

I don't know how she does it, because my own heart is back to its gymnastics routine, but good old Margaret plays it cool.

"Oh! Hi! Winnie! How are you? These are my par-ents. Mom, Dad, this is Winifred Winterbottom. She used to work for Miss Harriman."

Winnie nods at Mr. and Mrs. Wrobel, and then some-thing really strange happens. Winnie smiles. Yep, you read that right. Winnie smiles. Okay, so she's not going to challenge Raf's position at the top of the list of World's Greatest Smiles, but it's real, and it has an effect on me that I wouldn't have thought possible: it makes her seem . . . human.

"I am doing very well, thank you. Many changes in

my life since I left Miss Elizabeth, some good, some not so good, but I'm still here."

"We, um, heard about you and Mr. Winterbottom," Margaret says. "I'm sorry."

Winnie's smile fades as she nods at Margaret. "Yes, thank you. Twenty-six years we are together. Well, I must return to work. It was good to see you girls again. Be sure to tell Miss Elizabeth I said hello."

When she's out of hearing range, Margaret turns to me. "Well, that's that. We have to get them back together."

"Winnie and Elizabeth? I don't know, Margaret. Elizabeth seems pretty happy with Helen. And remember, she said Winnie was a lousy housekeeper."

"Not Winnie and Elizabeth. Winnie and Gordon. You saw her face when I mentioned him. She misses him. And it's almost Christmas. They can't spend the holidays apart."

I try my hardest, but no matter what I do, I just can't wrap my mind around the concept of missing Gordon Winterbottom. Apparently, there are still some ideas too foreign for my brain to process.

"But . . . why? They're probably better off without each other."

Even as I say it, I know I'm wasting my breath; once an idea takes root in Margaret's brain, there's no turning back. The girl could teach your average mule a thing or two about being stubborn.

Chapter 11

In which Mr. Eliot uses real magic to battle the Nine Worthy Men

Mr. Eliot, or, as we now refer to him, King George the Unfair, has scheduled (can you believe it?) a Saturday-morning rehearsal of *The Merry Gentlemen,* so Margaret and I meet Leigh Ann, Becca, and Livvy at Coffeeteria.

Wait! Don't leave! I know what you're thinking: Sophie talks a big game about saving Perkatory, but here she is, a few days later, feasting with the enemy.

Let me explain.

When Leigh Ann first suggested it as a meeting place, I went ballistic, but then I started to think about it. If Perkatory is going to reopen (and survive), they need to know their competition. As far as I'm concerned, it's not breakfast: it's a spy mission. The way I see it, I owe it to Perkatory to check out Coffeeteria.

The first thing I notice is how clean the place is. Practically sterile. It smells more like disinfectant than coffee, and my shoes squeak on the shiny floors, something that has never happened at Perkatory. But it's clear to me immediately that the place has no soul. Coffeeteria is corporate, overproduced pop music, while Perk is gritty, in-your-face punk. Where would you rather go?

While my friends marvel at the variety of pastries and coffee flavors, I'm already busy plotting the overthrow of this impostor, with its generic "Happy Holidays" decorations hanging from the ceiling. "This is no coffee shop. Coffee shops are supposed to have mismatched, secondhand furniture. This place looks like the lobby of a four-star hotel."

"I don't know—it seems pretty nice to me," says Leigh Ann.

"I have to agree with her," says Livvy. "At least I'm not, um, afraid to sit on these chairs. That one couch at Perk—"

"I know, I know. Perkatory's not the cleanest place. But I still don't believe they have rats."

"Sophie, the health inspector saw one," Margaret reminds me. "How do you explain that?"

"I can't—yet. But Raf and I are working on it."

Livvy elbows me gently, grinning. "Working on it, eh? Sounds serious."

"Yeah, I'll bet there's really a lot of work going on there," says Becca, who turns and heads for a table before I have a chance to respond.

The rest of us join her a few seconds later, and then

the serious evaluation begins. The coffee, we decide, is too strong for our taste, and the pastries are huge but otherwise nothing special. The hot chocolate, however (and it practically kills me to admit this), is delicious. Spectacular, even.

As our discussion continues, the manager stops by our table. "Good morning, girls. You're up bright and early on a Saturday morning. How is everything? Can I get you a free refill on those coffees?"

"No thank you," Leigh Ann replies. "I'm okay. Everything is great. The hot chocolate is fantastic."

He beams. "Wonderful. Well, if you need anything, let me know."

The whole time he's there in front of me, I'm scowling at him and watching his pockets for signs of small furry critters.

"We usually go to Perkatory," I say. "We've been going there for years. I can't wait until they reopen."

My friends' jaws all hit the table as I'm talking, but the manager—Jeff, according to his name tag—doesn't bat an eye.

"Yes, well, I heard they had some problems. I'm sure they'll take care of everything. But I hope to see you back here." He reaches into his vest pocket and takes out four coupons for free small coffees—and that's when I see a tiny pink nose and whiskers. Raf is right! I pretend to be interested in the coupons he's handing Margaret, but I watch secretly as his hand immediately

110

returns to his pocket and gently pushes his four-legged friend back where he belongs.

Even when he's gone, I keep my little secret. I smell a rat, all right, and his name is Jeff.

Rehearsal for *The Merry Gentlemen*—or, as it is known to us, *The Merry, but Constantly Changing and Evolving Gentlemen*—ends at noon. Mr. Eliot has finally agreed to stop making changes, which is a good thing, because we have exactly six days to pull the darn thing together.

We wait until everybody else is gone to approach him about a plan that Margaret and I cooked up in a post-Heidelberg flurry of deep thinking. German food can do that to you.

I dig into the very depths of my being, searching for a level of charm that I've never accessed before. I take a deep breath and throw out my first pitch, slow and right over the middle of the plate. "So, Mr. Eliot, how's it going? I think this play is really coming together, don't you?"

He's closing the curtain and turning off lights, and when I note the dumbstruck look on his face, I keep going.

"You know, I've always wanted to try writing a play, but I just don't think I have what it takes. But the way you took those characters from the Dickens story and turned them into something—"

"Stop!" He holds up his hands as if I'm mugging him. "What do you want, St. Pierre? Money? My wallet?"

"Why, whatever are you talking about, Mr. Eliot? I was merely hoping that you might consider sharing some of your vast knowledge."

Behind me, Becca and Leigh Ann snicker. Perhaps I *have* laid it on a bit thick.

"Oh, puh-leeeez!" he exclaims. "Seriously, my own mother doesn't pour it on like that. So, what do you girls want? You want me to talk to Sister Bernadette about a cast party after the show?"

Margaret steps up to bat. (Sorry, I'm not sure what is going on with all these baseball metaphors.) "Welllll, since you're asking, there is one little favor you could do for us. What are you doing right now—the next hour or so? We wouldn't want you to change your plans with Mrs. Eliot or anything like that."

He checks his watch. "I have a little time; what's the favor? Nothing illegal, I trust."

"Absolutely not," says Margaret. "Cross my heart. All you have to do is come with us up to Eighty-First Street, to a used-book store called Sturm & Drang."

"I know the place." He eyes us suspiciously. "Why there? Why me?"

"Well, you weren't our first choice, to be honest," I admit. "We were going to ask Malcolm Chance, but the guy at the bookstore knows him. He was with us at the auction."

"Auction?" He's shaking his head with a what-have-they-gotten-themselves-into-this-time look on his face.

"Don't worry. Margaret will explain it all later."

"Here's the plan," says Margaret. "You go in the bookstore while we wait outside, out of sight. If he sees us, he'll know something is up."

"I'm sure you're going to explain to me why he is so suspicious of you, right?"

Margaret ignores him. "With all your theater experience, you're up for a little acting, aren't you? Here's your part: you are a rare-book collector, and you're just browsing. After a few minutes, make your way back toward the counter. You'll see a cabinet with glass doors—that's where he keeps all the good stuff. Inside, there's a copy of *The Mill on the Floss* by George Eliot." When she sees the face he makes, she pauses, remembering that Mr. Eliot's first name is George. "Oh, right, I guess you would know that one."

"Yes, I would," he says.

"That book is listed on the website for twelve hundred dollars. Just say that you saw it online and might be interested. Here's a printout of the page from his site. Then, as you hand that book back to him, something else in the cabinet is going to catch your eye. It's a set of books called *Nine Worthy Men,* three volumes in a slipcase, in very nice condition. Are you with me so far? Good. Because next comes the tricky part. Look carefully at the first volume in the set. There's one of those built-in bookmarks, a piece of red ribbon. We want you to . . . tug on that ribbon and see what happens."

"Excuse me?"

"I know it sounds crazy, but once we tell you the rest of the story, you'll see. When the guy from the shop hands you that book, we're going to come in and create a little distraction so you can do what you need to do."

"What do you think is going to happen when I pull on that ribbon? Is it going to summon Charlemagne's ghost or something equally dramatic? What if it comes all the way out? What am I supposed to do then?"

"How did you know Charlemagne was one of them?" I ask.

Mr. Eliot taps his forehead. "There's a whole warehouse full of useless information up here, St. Pierre."

Margaret takes an eight-inch piece of red ribbon from her bag. "I've got it covered."

Mr. Eliot looks at our waiting faces. "I still want to hear the rest of this story, but fine, okay, let's go. I reserve the right to reconsider."

"So you'll really do it?" Becca asks, not hiding the surprise in her voice. "I bet them you wouldn't."

"Sorry to disappoint you, Miss Chen."

"We'll see," she says. "The opera ain't over till it's over."

But he doesn't change his mind, even after hearing the rest of the story on the subway ride to Eighty-Sixth Street. We stop a few doors down from Sturm & Drang for a quick review of the plan. Mr. Eliot checks his coat pocket one final time for the piece of red ribbon and the folded paper with the information that Margaret printed out from Marcus Klinger's website, and then he's off.

Once he's inside, we scurry down the sidewalk to the near corner of the bookstore's front window and crouch into spying position, ready to pounce the second we see him crack open *Nine Worthy Men*.

For a used-book store in an out-of-the-way location, Sturm & Drang is strangely busy; there are three other people in the store besides Mr. Eliot, and Marcus Klinger moves from customer to customer, chatting and smiling—things he never bothered to do for us. Mr. Eliot discovers the Dickens shelf, and spends a long time leafing through a copy of *David Copperfield*.

"What is he doing?" Becca asks.

"He totally forgot why he's in there," groans Leigh Ann. "Look, now he's reading that huge book. He'll be in that shop forever. Man, he is such a dork."

"Relax," Margaret assures us. "He knows what he's doing."

"Now I'm sure we're in trouble," says Becca.

My legs start to cramp as Mr. Eliot continues reading. Just as I'm starting to think Becca and Leigh Ann are right, he closes *David Copperfield*—a bit reluctantly, I think—and makes his move toward the locked glass cabinet. He unfolds the paper and checks it, looks at the books, and then back at the paper.

Klinger approaches, glancing at the paper in Mr.

Eliot's hand. We can't hear the conversation through the glass, but everything seems to be going according to plan. Mr. Eliot shows him the paper, on which he has circled the crucial details about the other George Eliot's masterpiece. Klinger nods enthusiastically at something Mr. Eliot says, unlocks the cabinet, and hands him *The Mill on the Floss*.

"I don't think Klinger asked him if his hands were clean," I whisper to Margaret.

Mr. Eliot examines the book so carefully that I start to believe he's actually going to buy it. Klinger wanders off to help someone else for a moment and when he returns, Mr. Eliot hands him the book with a shake of his head and points at something else in the cabinet.

"Here we go," says Margaret as Klinger reaches for the slipcased set of *Nine Worthy Men*. "Everybody ready?"

The rest of us grunt at her. "It's about time," Becca complains. "I can't feel my toes. If we have to make a run for it, I'm in big trouble."

Mr. Eliot is opening the first volume as we burst through the door, talking noisily.

"Why are we going in here again?" Becca says loudly.

"Yeah, Sophie, I thought you said you would never sell him that pen," Leigh Ann adds.

"Maybe I've changed my mind," I say. "Five hundred bucks would buy me a lot of books. We could buy that copy of *A Christmas Carol*."

We walk past Mr. Eliot without a look and head for the farthest corner of the store, where we all start pulling books from the shelves willy-nilly.

Our little plan works perfectly. The mere sight of four street urchins with their grubby little fingers all over his precious books sends Marcus Klinger into an absolute tizzy. He rushes to the back of the store to deal with us, leaving Mr. Eliot alone with *Nine Worthy Men*.

"Young ladies!" he cries. "Please, be gentle! This is not a thrift shop! These are valuable antiques, and must be handled properly. If you want to see something, I would greatly prefer that you ask me to show it to you. Please."

I know he's only being nice to us because there are other customers in the shop and because he wants my dad's fountain pen. The soupçon of hope that I may be reconsidering has worked a small miracle on his disposition.

As he's showing Becca the proper way to turn the pages in an old book, I glide a few feet down the aisle until I can see Mr. Eliot. He glances around the shop, looking very nervous and trying to determine where Klinger is. When he's finally satisfied that Klinger is occupied with helping us, he closes his eyes and gives the red ribbon a healthy tug. His eyes open wide as a few more inches of ribbon come out from somewhere inside the binding. He pulls again, and even more ribbon appears. The look in his eyes tells me that he's starting to panic as he's suddenly holding on to two feet of ribbon.

"Keep pulling!" I hiss at him.

So he pulls. And pulls. And pulls some more. I have to cover my mouth to prevent myself from laughing at the look on his face as the red ribbon simply keeps coming: he looks like a magician who has just realized he really can perform magic. As one hand keeps yanking yards and yards of ribbon from the binding, the other is busy scooping and wrapping and cramming long loops of the stuff into his coat pocket.

Behind me, I hear Klinger making noises like he's finished lecturing Margaret, Leigh Ann, and Becca, and is about to return to the front counter.

"Hey, mister, how much is this book?" I shout, waving a copy of *Sense and Sensibility*. And then, in Mr. Eliot's direction, I hiss, "Hurry!"

"I'm coming, I'm coming," Klinger says, exasperated. "Really, you girls need to learn some proper etiquette if you're going to continue to come in my store. Now, what do you want to know?"

He starts talking about the book while I look past him at Mr. Eliot, who has pulled out a good twenty feet of ribbon and looks like he might drop dead any second.

And then . . . abracadabra, presto chango! He reaches the end of the ribbon, and something truly miraculous occurs! As he pulls the final few inches free and they drop to the floor, a perfect replacement ribbon is left in place, attached to the binding just as the original had been. He won't even need Margaret's piece of ribbon!

Mr. Eliot stuffs the last few feet into his pocket, and takes a much-needed deep breath. Gently, he slides the volume into place in the slipcase and takes one step back from the counter just as Klinger reappears.

"It's quite a set," says Mr. Eliot. "I've, uh, never seen anything like it. You're sure it's not for sale?"

Klinger rubs his chin. "Not right now, anyway. Maybe one day. Keep your eye on the website after the first of the year. If I change my mind, I'll list it there."

"Fair enough," says Mr. Eliot, shaking his hand and making his way toward the door. "Nice little place you have here. Pity about those . . . little hooligans." He pulls the door closed behind him.

Hooligans!

Chapter 12

I guess that's one way to make a gluten-free pizza

According to our plan, we're supposed to wait in the store five minutes after Mr. Eliot leaves, so it doesn't look too suspicious. Well, let me tell you, it is the longest five minutes of my life—keeping quiet about what I have just witnessed.

When the door clangs shut behind us, I run until I'm several doors down from Sturm & Drang, where I collapse onto the frozen ground in a fit of laughter. Margaret, Becca, and Leigh Ann look on, not at all sure what to think of their friend, who, it appears, has lost her mind.

Becca, naturally, is first to comment. "I knew this day would come. She's completely cracked. Around the bend. Checked out. Bonkers. Loony."

"You didn't see his face," I say, pulling myself together. "It just kept coming and coming. Like one of those magician's handkerchiefs."

"What kept coming? The ribbon?" Margaret asks. "How much came out?"

"Miles," I say. "Miles and miles. He's pulling and pulling and trying to stuff it in his pockets, and—" I completely lose it again.

"She's mental," says Leigh Ann, checking her watch. "And we'd better get moving or Mr. Eliot is going to ditch us."

Margaret and Leigh Ann pull me to my feet, and we find Mr. Eliot waiting inside the bodega at the corner, just as we had arranged.

"Remind me," he says, calmly pouring himself a cup of coffee, "never to listen to you girls again. I almost had a heart attack in there! And you, Miss St. Pierre—fat lot of help you were. 'Hurry! Hurry!' you say. What if he had come back and seen me with half a mile of ribbon wrapped around me?"

"We're sorry, really," says Margaret, trying to hold in a smile. "We didn't know. Honest. That's why we needed the diversion. Now, can we see this ribbon?"

Mr. Eliot hands me the end of the ribbon. "Show them what they missed."

I re-create the moment, doing my best imitation of Mr. Eliot freaking out. It's a wasted performance, though, because they've discovered that there's writing on the ribbon and are desperately trying to read it as I yank it out of Mr. Eliot's pocket.

"What does it say?" Mr. Eliot asks.

"I'll bet it's secret plans for building nukes," says Becca, who sees conspiracies everywhere. (She's convinced that the long-awaited and still-ongoing Second Avenue subway project is a cover story while the government digs up an alien race of pod people before they have a chance to take over the planet.)

"It's just a string of hundreds of letters, on both sides. I can't make out any words at all. It's got to be a code." As Margaret runs her fingers the length of the ribbon, she is getting that go-ahead-and-try-to-outsmart-me-old-man look in her eyes. "Well, I think it's also safe to say that we are pretty darn good at cracking codes."

Sleepover night at my apartment means two things when the RBGDA is on a case: we're going to stuff ourselves on Dad's latest culinary creation and then stay awake until we solve whatever problem we're facing.

Imagine our disappointment, then, when we learn that Dad forgot to cook for us. No *poulet au vinaigre*. No macaroni *et fromage*. Not even a box of day-old pastries.

Leigh Ann is taking it hardest. She sits at our table, gazing forlornly at the oven that has brought her so much happiness over the past few months.

"Bummer," says Becca.

"I've been looking forward to this all day," says Leigh Ann. "All week."

"Sorry. Look, we'll just order something. I even have

a coupon for this new pizza place—Crazy Ray's. Buy one, get one free. How can you go wrong with a deal like that?"

"I'm not so sure, Sophie," Margaret cautions. "Let's stick with something we know, like Trantonno's? Or Famous Ray's? Or Luciano's, where your blue-eyed boyfriend works. Maybe he'll even deliver it. At least with one of those, we'll know what we're getting."

"He's not my boyfriend," I say as I call the number on the coupon.

Turns out there's a good reason Crazy Ray's pizza is so cheap: it is just plain awful.

"This is worse than school cafeteria pizza," Becca declares, prying her third slice loose from the box. "I can't tell where the crust ends and the cardboard begins."

Leigh Ann sighs heavily. "I think the crust *is* cardboard."

"It doesn't seem to be slowing Rebecca down," notes Margaret.

Becca shrugs. "Bad pizza is still pizza."

"Well, there's a whole pie left, and I don't think anyone is going to fight you for it," I say.

Dad comes into the kitchen with his coat on, ready to leave for the restaurant, and instantly that noble schnoz of his starts sniffing like mad. "What is that terrible smell?" He opens the lid of the second pizza box. "Yeeouughhh. What is this? This is not pizza. *Quelle horreur!* This is a . . . disgrace to the good name of pizza.

Sophie! Do not tell me that you bought this horrible stuff for your friends! This is how you treat your guests?"

My so-called friends turn and glare at me.

"See?" says Leigh Ann. "It doesn't even smell like good pizza."

"It's your fault," I say, pointing at Dad, who is shocked by my pronouncement.

"*Excusez-moi?* My fault, you say?"

"It's not your fault," Leigh Ann explains. "It's just that usually, when we come over to spend the night with Sophie, you cook something amazing for us."

"Ahhh. Now I see. I'm sorry, girls, but I promise—I will make it up to you. A true feast."

"Yay!" shouts Leigh Ann.

"Now, please make that go away," he says, giving the leftover pizza a dismissive wave on his way out the kitchen door.

"Wait! Dad, don't leave!" I shout. "I have a question for you. Just a second, it's in my backpack." I run to my room and return with the empty wine bottle from Mr. Dedmann's, which I hold up for Dad to see.

"*Mon Dieu,*" he whispers. "*Château Latour. Quarante-neuf.* Where did you get this?"

Well, this is awkward. Dad doesn't know about Shelley or Mr. Dedmann, and the explanation would take too long.

"Um, from this woman we met who is, um, trying to sort out this collection of stuff she inherited. Kind of a long story. Boring, really. So, what's the deal with this wine? Is it any good?"

Hoo-boy, was that the wrong question to ask.

"Is it any good?" he repeats, flabbergasted by my ignorance. "One might as well ask if the ceiling of the Sistine Chapel is pretty. Or if Mozart's music is nice. Sophie, this is not merely wine; this is poetry in a bottle. Château Latour isn't good; it is . . . sublime. And that is in a bad year. But 1949 was one of the best vintages in history." He sniffs the inside of the bottle and smiles. *"Très magnifique."*

"So, what's this stuff worth?" Becca asks.

Dad purses his lips and considers the question. "A bottle of 'this stuff,' as you say, would sell for six to eight thousand dollars. Possibly a bit more."

That sound you just heard? Four chins hitting the floor.

"Eight thousand dollars! For one bottle of wine!" Becca exclaims. "No way. Nobody would pay that. It's ridiculous. You're kidding, right?"

Becca, Becca, Becca. Dad doesn't kid about wine. He gives her his special version of "the stink-eye" and assures her that he is quite serious.

"B-b-but why?" she blubbers.

"Some people demand the very best," he answers. "And this—this is the best. Also, as you can imagine, there are very few bottles left from 1949."

"Doesn't it, you know, go bad after all that time?" Leigh Ann asks.

"Not if it is stored properly," Dad says.

"Like in a wine cellar?" Margaret asks.

"*Oui*. A wine cellar. Does your . . . friend have more bottles like this? With the wine still inside, perhaps?"

"We'll have to get back to you on that," I say.

Margaret takes out her notebook and shows Dad the note she copied from inside the one on Dedmann's desk:

WILL TO GA
SI ROTH
SS VOUG
OS FIG

"Just out of curiosity, does this mean anything to you?" she asks. "Maybe something to do with wine?"

Dad stares at the paper for a few seconds. "No, it— Wait, yes, it makes sense. Except for the first line. The rest, though, is easy. The first two aren't letters, they're numbers. The five looks like an 'S.' 'Fifty-one Roth,' that's a 1951 Rothschild. And a fifty-five Vougeot. The last one is a 2005 Figeac. These are all very good wines."

"Wait a minute," I say. "Good, like the stuff you and Mom drink, or good, like eight thousand dollars?"

"Somewhere in between," he says. "But closer to the second thing you said."

After the excitement over the eight thousand–dollar bottle of wine wears off, Margaret unrolls all twenty-seven feet of ribbon that Mr. Eliot pulled from *Nine Worthy*

Men. She passes it through her fingers, examining it inch by inch.

"Okay, we pulled the ribbon, just like the instructions said. What does he mean, 'the walking stick is the key'?"

"I'll bet there's a secret compartment in Dedmann's walking stick, and Klinger knows about it. If it has that, and he knows that it's the key to those floor thingies, we're toast."

Margaret doesn't even hear me; she presses her fingertips into her temples and drifts off to the happy thinking place deep down in her scary brain. "The code says that the stick *is* the key, not the stick holds the key. But either way, we need that stick."

"Well, we could ask Mr. Eliot—"

"UNLESS!" Margaret shouts, interrupting the guaranteed-to-be-profound thought I'm about to express. She leaps to her feet and runs out of my room.

Becca, Leigh Ann, and I stare at each other. "Where do you suppose she's going?" Becca finally asks.

Before I can answer, Margaret returns with a broom.

"I knew it," Leigh Ann says. "Margaret is a wizard, isn't she? That explains so much! How long have you guys known?"

"Yeah, I guess it's time you heard the truth," I say. "I've known for three years now. Margaret can fly."

Margaret is too busy wrapping the ribbon around the broomstick to listen to what we're saying. "Sophie, come here. Put your finger right here, on the end of the ribbon."

"What are you doing?"

"The walking stick is the key," she repeats, continuing to wind the ribbon around the broomstick. "It's called a scytale, an ancient system for sending messages in code. It was used by the Greeks—people like Hector, and maybe even Alexander the Great. It makes perfect sense!"

"How does it work?" Leigh Ann asks over my shoulder.

"It's incredibly simple, really," Margaret explains, "as long as you have a stick that's the right diameter. If you want to write a secret message, you take the blank ribbon and wrap it around the stick like I'm doing, then you write your message across all those wraps of ribbon. Then you just fill in all the extra space with random letters, unwrap it, and send it to somebody who has a stick just like the one you used to create the message. They wrap it around theirs, and they can read what you wrote. Obviously, Dedmann used his walking stick."

"What if this broomstick isn't the same size as his walking stick?" I ask.

"Then it won't work," Margaret says. "But I'm prepared for that, too."

Three feet of the broomstick is completely covered by the ribbon by the time Margaret finishes wrapping. Leigh Ann holds the other loose end of ribbon as Margaret searches for the secret message.

"Anything?" I ask.

"Not yet."

"You know, I saw that walking stick today when we were in Klinger's shop," says Leigh Ann, "and it's definitely fatter than this. It looks really heavy."

Margaret unwinds the ribbon. "That's okay. I have a Plan B. Sophie, get me today's newspaper. And some tape—any kind will do."

"Aye, aye." I'm back with the paper and a roll of Scotch tape in seconds. "What's all this about?"

Margaret unfolds the newspaper, making a stack of single sheets of newsprint. She starts with a double thickness of pages from the arts section and wraps it around the broomstick again and again. I tear off a piece of tape to hold the edge of the paper in place.

Margaret shows the finished product to Leigh Ann. "What do you think?"

"A little thicker. I think."

Two more sheets of newspaper go on, and we all turn to Leigh Ann to see her reaction.

"You're making me nervous," she says. "I only saw it for a second. That looks pretty close to me."

That's good enough for Margaret, who starts winding ribbon again, and who starts smiling before she even gets to the end.

"There! Do you see it?" She reads:

> Beware the Ides of March, a prophet said,
> Which he ignored, and now he's dead.
> His medallion is the first of three,
> Clockwise turned with the key.

Okay, future detectives, here's another question for you. This one, however, is too easy for multiple choice:

Based on the information in this poem, whose medallion is the first of three?

Do I really need to warn you about peeking ahead?

Chapter 13

You should see what he makes me on Valentine's Day

"Julius Caesar!" Margaret, Leigh Ann, and I shout out simultaneously.

Becca just looks bewildered. "Man, you guys are geeks. How do you know that?"

"Oh, come on, Becca," I say. "You've never heard 'Beware the Ides of March' before? March fifteenth? The day Julius Caesar was assassinated? My dad even makes me a special breakfast on that day. It's a giant stack of pancakes with a knife stuck in the middle, and strawberry syrup oozing out of the wound. Because, you know, Julius Caesar was—"

"I get it, I get it," says Becca. "I know how he was killed, I just didn't know exactly when."

"So is it the same message on the other side?" Leigh Ann asks.

Margaret looks at her, puzzled. "Other side?" And then it hits her. "The other side of the ribbon! I almost

131

forgot. We have to check the letters on that side, too. But, first, we have to write this message down."

She jots it down in a notebook, double-checking every letter of every word, and then unwinds the ribbon from the broomstick. As she rewinds the ribbon with the "back" side showing, the rest of us are competing to be first to spot the secret message.

"Hey, I see it!" I shout as Margaret winds the last few inches of ribbon onto the stick. "Let me read it."

> The walls proclaim mankind's best,
> To find your Muse is the second test.
> As the view of Delft was revealed to him,
> Shall his eyes to you in a chamber dim,
> Divulge her name and the final quest.

Everyone else takes a good look to make sure I haven't missed anything, and once that message is copied in Margaret's notebook, she wonders aloud, "What should we do with the ribbon?"

"Keep it secret. Keep it safe," Becca says, quoting Gandalf. "It must not fall into the enemy's hands."

"We might as well hide it here," says Margaret. "Sophie, where's your best hiding spot?"

"Yeah, Soph, where do you keep all your deepest secrets?" Becca asks, poking around my desk.

"Get away from there," I say. "If I told you, it wouldn't be secret anymore, would it?"

"So you're admitting that you do keep secrets from us," says Becca. "In-teresting."

"Just give me the ribbon. I'll hide it after you leave, Becca. So, now what?" I ask.

"Well, Julius Caesar is our 'worthy man'; there's no doubt about that. Now we have to find ourselves a Muse," answers Margaret, glancing at the two poems written in her notebook. "And we know for sure that we were right about the medallions. They're all part of one big lock."

"And we're going to need that walking stick to turn the medallions," Leigh Ann says. "Don't forget that."

"What about the second poem?" I ask. "Anybody have any ideas? 'As the view of Delft was revealed to him.' What's Delft?"

"Jeez, Sophie. I can't believe you don't know that," says Becca. "It's a city, someplace in Europe. I thought everyone knew that."

"Okay, okay. I'm sorry about that Ides of March crack," I say. "How do you know about Delft?"

"The *View of Delft* is a painting by Vermeer. We studied it in my art class when we were talking about perspective. It's one of those paintings . . . You know, at first, I'm thinking, 'Meh—this is nothing special. Just another landscape.' But the longer you look at it, the more you start to see."

Margaret's fingers are pressed against her temples as her mighty brain focuses like a laser beam on the poem before her. "The name of the Muse is going to be revealed to us . . . as the *View of Delft* was revealed to

Vermeer. What does that mean? Rebecca, you're the artist. How is a painting revealed to a painter? How do you decide what goes into the picture?"

Becca shrugs. "I dunno, you just . . . know, I guess. But one of my teachers did teach me a little trick that's amazing for landscapes. He takes this big piece of mat board with a little rectangle cut out of the middle. Then he holds it up and looks through the hole at the scene he's thinking about painting. He just keeps moving it around—side to side, close and far—until he, you know, finds the picture he wants to paint."

"Hmmm," says Margaret. "There must be some other way of looking at the poem. I just need to sleep on it. That always helps. I know it's a radical idea, but I was thinking that maybe we could try to go to sleep at a reasonable hour tonight."

Well, we could.

We probably should.

But . . . well, we all know better, don't we?

The lights finally go out a little after midnight, and we settle into sleeping positions for the night. Our heads are together in the center of the floor, with our bodies stretched out like the spokes of a wheel. For a few quiet moments, we stare at the glow-in-the-dark stars that Margaret helped me stick to the ceiling. (Because Margaret was involved, you can bet your sweet Betelgeuse that each one is right where it should be, astronomically speaking.)

"When I was little," says Leigh Ann, "we visited some relatives way out in the country in the Dominican Republic, and I swear, that's how the stars looked. I felt like I could just reach up and touch them. . . . It was so beautiful."

"Doesn't this remind you of the first time all four of us had a sleepover?" I ask. "Remember? It was the night we found the Ring of Rocamadour, and Elizabeth insisted that we keep it overnight?"

"And how we passed it back and forth during the night, without even realizing that we were doing it?" Margaret adds. "Kind of hard to forget."

"Hard to believe that was only a few months ago," says Becca. "It seems like L.A. has been part of the gang forever."

"Does everyone remember what they wished for that night?" I ask.

According to the legend of the Ring of Rocamadour, St. Veronica appears in the dreams of the person wearing the ring and answers her prayers. "I remember mine: I wished for the four of us to stay friends forever. I think we're doing okay, don't you? You're all wearing your rings, right?"

Each of us has a perfect copy of the Ring of Rocamadour, a thank-you from Elizabeth Harriman for finding the ring, and for reuniting her with daughter Caroline and granddaughter Caitlin. We've made a solemn vow to wear them every day for the rest of our lives. We are, as Becca constantly reminds us, ring-bearers—just like Frodo.

"Of course," says Becca.

"Every day," says Margaret.

"I've never taken it off my finger," says Leigh Ann. "You guys may not realize this, but that was the best night of my life—it still is. Before I transferred to St. V's, I never had friends like you, who were smart, and funny, and nice. Even you, Sophie, when you thought I liked Raf. Well, maybe for a few days there, you weren't so nice. Anyway, I remember what everybody wished for that night. Margaret, you wished you could relive your eighth birthday with your grandfather, back in Poland. I wanted my parents to get back together. Fat chance of that happening now that my dad lives in Cleveland. And, Rebecca, you wanted to see your dad again, even if it was only in your dreams. I'll always remember that, because you said you could still smell the ink from his print shop, but you'd stopped dreaming about him. I cried for like an hour after you guys went to sleep that night just thinking about it."

We're quiet for a long time after that.

Becca finally breaks the silence. "You know what I'd wish for right now?"

"What?" we all ask, waiting breathlessly.

"Some more of that pizza. I'm kinda hungry."

I don't care if we did make a vow to be friends for life; I wind up and thump her with my pillow as hard as I can. Within seconds, Margaret and Leigh Ann have joined in the beating.

On Sunday afternoon, it's just Margaret and me again. Leigh Ann is off to Queens to go shopping with her mom, and Becca is meeting some of her "artistic friends" at the Metropolitan Museum to attend an exhibit of paintings by some Dutch guy I've never heard of.

I meet Margaret outside her building, where she announces, "First stop, Mr. Dedmann's cellar. We need to get a good look at the Vermeer medallion. If Rebecca's right about the name of that painting, the poem must have something to do with him."

"Um, yeah, that sounds good. Hey, um, sorry to change the subject, but what do you think happened to Dedmann's dog after he died?" I ask. "I started thinking about that last night. I'm still hoping that my parents will let me get one."

"That's a good question," Margaret says. "I'm sure Shelley will know."

When we get to Dedmann's house, I ring the bell and my question is answered before Shelley even opens the door: inside the house, a dog is barking at us.

"Come in, come in," Shelley says. "She's very friendly. Her name is Bertie, with a 't.' Personally, I think she ought to be Birdie with a 'd,' because she loves to chase them."

My knees hit the floor and she buries her head in my coat, tail wagging nonstop.

"Oh my gosh. She is so beautiful. I think I'm in love." I look up at Margaret and flutter my eyelashes. "Can I keep her? Can I?"

She shakes her head. "No, you cannot keep her."

"Actually," Shelley says, "you could. I'm looking for a good home for her. I would love to keep her myself, but if I found the right home for her . . . She's a great dog, and she's only about eighteen months old. She is something like the seventeenth English setter that Mr. Dedmann owned. Are you serious about wanting a dog?"

"Oh, I'm plenty serious," I say. "It's my parents who are the problem. I haven't convinced them yet."

Margaret and Shelley both start to speak at the same time: "I have some big news—"

Laughing, Shelley says, "You first."

"Sophie showed that wine bottle to her dad."

"And?"

Margaret can't contain her smile. "Six to eight thousand dollars. Can you believe it?"

Shelley's reaction is the same as ours was: her mouth opens, but she's unable to speak for a moment. "Wh-what?" She has to sit on the upholstered bench in the foyer. "What if . . . What if there's more? A lot more.

That must be the secret Mr. Dedmann was talking about. The answers to all the questions."

"I don't get why he didn't just tell you the combination," I say. "He left it to you in his will, but then doesn't tell you how to get to it. Crazy."

"Maybe not so crazy," says Margaret. "Mr. Dedmann must have had a good reason for holding this secret so close to his chest. Now, what was your big news?"

"Oh! Yes! Follow me," Shelley says. "After you left the other day, I got to thinking. There was one other strange thing that happened with Mr. Dedmann a few months before he died. I watched him go down the spiral stairs into the cellar room one morning, like he often did. But then, a few minutes later, I ran into him right here in this hallway. The funny thing is, I was at a bookcase by the spiral staircase the whole time, and I never saw him come up. I was walking toward the kitchen, and suddenly, there he was."

"And you're sure you didn't miss him coming up the stairs?" Margaret asks.

"It would have been impossible. He was in his nineties, and he moved rather slowly, as you can imagine. At the time, I was busy, and didn't give it another thought. But then, after we talked, I started thinking about it. The only reasonable conclusion is that there must be another way to the basement. And that's when I found this." She leads us into a little breakfast nook in the kitchen, situated at the back of the house. Reaching behind a small light fixture mounted on the wall, Shelley pushes a button and a section of paneling on the side wall, identical to the others around it, pops open.

"A dumbwaiter!" says Margaret, opening the door the rest of the way. "It's a small elevator, really!"

I take a look inside. "Kinda scary. Have you . . . taken it down to the cellar?"

Shelley shakes her head. "I was afraid to, because I'm the only one here. If it got stuck—"

"Smart," says Margaret. "Don't worry, Sophie and I will test it for you."

We will? I haven't had the best luck with elevators lately. Inside, I'm screaming at Margaret: HAVE YOU LOST YOUR MIND!?

"Come on, Soph. We need to go down there, anyway, remember?" She explains to Shelley, "We solved the first part of the combination, and we have the clue for part two, but we need to get a good look at the Vermeer medallion."

"Do you even know how this thing works?" I ask, squeezing in next to Margaret.

"I think I'll start with this button that points down," she says. "See you in the cellar, Shelley!"

The door closes, leaving us in complete blackness. There's a slight jar, and then we start the v-e-r-y s-l-o-w downward journey.

I use light from my phone to illuminate Margaret's face. "Are you sure we're still moving?"

Before she answers, another shudder tells me that we've reached our destination. The door slides open, but we're facing a solid wall. "Now what?" I ask, lighting up the control panel, which consists of exactly two buttons: up and down.

"Push," says Margaret, her hands against the wall.

And just like that, the wall swings open with a long *crrreeeaakkkkkkkkk,* and we're in the cellar, where Shelley greets us with a relieved smile.

"Well, I could live my entire life without doing that again," I say.

Margaret is busy examining the medallion on the panel that hides the dumbwaiter. It belongs to Isaac Newton, which I suppose makes sense. (Elevator, gravity—get it?)

"Hey, look at this," she says. "Watch what happens when I spin the ring." The ring around Newton's face has nine apple-shaped cutouts, and when Margaret starts to spin it, the latch that holds the paneling shut starts to move. When she changes direction, the latch goes back into its original position.

"Try closing the door and then see if you can open it," I suggest.

"Good idea." Margaret closes the door and spins the ring until the door is latched so tightly that it's impossible to tell that there is a door. Then she spins it the other direction—nine complete rotations—and the door pops open.

"Remarkable," says Shelley. "This house is just full of surprises."

Satisfied, Margaret breaks out a pocket-size notebook and pen, and moves around the room, glancing quickly at each of the thirty-six wall medallions and jotting down the names for future reference as Shelley and I look over her shoulder.

"William Shakespeare. Thank goodness he's here. Ludwig van Beethoven—well, naturally. Rembrandt van Rijn. Johannes Kepler. Charles Dickens. Mr. Eliot will be pleased to hear that. Brahms. Tolstoy. Michelangelo. Ah, here we are, Jan Vermeer."

"See anything strange about it?" I ask.

Margaret doesn't have the chance to answer, though, because we hear Bertie barking upstairs. "Blast!" says Shelley. "That will be that awful Mr. Klinger. I completely forgot about him. He comes every Sunday to work down here, getting things ready for their weekly Beethoven meeting. He mentioned that he'd be bringing Lindsay with him today."

Margaret's eyes widen. "Lindsay! I don't want her to know we're here. Can we hide in the elevator?"

"Um, uh, yes," says Shelley, not sure what to make of someone so young and yet so bold.

That's my Margaret, though. The girl is absolutely

fearless. She grabs me by the arm and drags me to Isaac Newton's medallion, where she spins the dial until the door pops open. We pile inside and Margaret tells Shelley, "Make sure the panel is closed all the way, and then just spin the ring counterclockwise until it stops."

"Got it," says Shelley. "You're in. Are you going up?"

"Not yet," says Margaret. "We're going to listen for a while. Meet you in the kitchen later."

"He only stays for a few minutes," Shelley says. "Usually, that is. I'll be waiting for you upstairs."

"How long are we going to stay here?" I ask, feeling a little claustrophobic. "What if they stay down here for a couple of hours? Can I use my phone for some light?"

"Yes, but make sure that the ringer is off. And Sophie?"

"Yeah?"

"Don't forget to breathe."

"Thanks."

Chapter 14

I don't know about you, but that sounds like a challenge to me

Their voices are surprisingly clear through the wall, which is one of those good news / bad news situations. It's good that we can hear every word, but bad because I don't know how long I can stay perfectly still and quiet in a shopping cart–size elevator. Remember how I mentioned that I haven't had the best of luck with elevators lately? It wasn't that long ago that I spent a few hours stuck in the one at St. Veronica's, you see. That one was cold and dark, and I was trapped with Livvy Klack, who was not one of my favorite people in the world at the time, but at least we could sit. Heck, we could even stretch out on the floor. That's not the case in this dumbwaiter: Margaret and I are shoulder to shoulder, and my heart is banging against my ribs so hard that I'm sure Klinger and Lindsay can hear every telltale beat.

"Okay, the coast is clear. You go first," says Klinger. "You asked for this meeting. You keep telling me that this is a once-in-a-lifetime story that you're chasing, but you never give me any details. And why all the secrecy? Couldn't this have waited until the club meeting?"

"Just listen to me, that's all I ask," says Lindsay. "There's no need to involve the other members in this. They would only complicate matters, and I think we have enough to deal with already. These girls—the Red Blazer Girls, they call themselves—are a bigger problem than you realize. They seem to have a habit of solving mysteries—especially old ones. Curtis Dedmann's story is right up their alley. I would not put it past these girls to figure out the combination. Are you willing to take that chance? Don't forget, Dedmann left the contents of the house to Shelley, and if she discovers what's behind these walls before we can force her out, well, I don't think you even want to imagine that little scenario."

"Shhh. Softly, please. We don't want to give her any ideas. But come now. Surely you're not seriously concerned. In two weeks, all this is going to belong to Beethoven's Nine—and that includes everything behind these walls. And I don't care how clever they think they are, they are never going to unlock Dedmann's secrets. And once we're in and Shelley is out, we'll get behind these walls even if it takes a bulldozer. Which it probably will, if I know Dedmann. This place is a fortress. Let's be serious. What makes you think these grammar school girls, these delinquents, are capable of outsmarting me? I'm a Harvard graduate, you know."

When he says "girls" like that, I have to bite my lip not to shout through the wall at him. Margaret and I are so close in the dumbwaiter that I feel her body tense up, too.

"Don't underestimate them, Marcus. My boss did, and look where he is. Lost his job, lost his wife, scratching out a living selling antiques."

"Well, they have one other problem," Klinger says. "Even if they do figure out the combination—a big if, if you ask me—they still need this." He taps something on the marble floor—and I picture him holding Dedmann's walking stick. "And I promise you, they're never going to get their clever little hands on it."

"We'll see. From what I hear, they're quite resourceful."

"What is your angle?" Klinger asks. "I still don't understand what you want from me. Because you're newer to the club than I, it's true that your share won't be quite as large as mine, but trust me, you're still going to be rich. Here, help me set up for the meeting. The Bordeaux glasses are in the cabinet behind you."

Over the clinking of wineglasses, Lindsay continues. "It's very simple, Marcus. All I'm asking for is your guarantee that I have exclusive rights to Mr. Dedmann's story, and to anything related to his past, like diaries, notebooks, photos. I . . . Well, let's just say that I have good reason to believe that they exist. If Shelley Gallivan finds them, they become her property. She'll auction them off, or they'll become part of the Curtis Dedmann museum or something similarly ridiculous, where anyone might have access to them. There will be ten books about Dedmann before you know it, and mine will get lost in the shuffle."

"But why would anyone want to read about him? What makes his story so interesting? Other than being a mechanical genius and having exquisite taste in wine, what is so special about Curtis Dedmann?"

"Because," says Lindsay, "if I'm right, Curtis Dedmann was the German spy known as the Third Wise Man, and I will be sitting on a story that has bestseller written all over it. Maybe even a Pulitzer Prize. My career, Marcus—that's what I want. Oh, don't get me wrong; the money will be nice, too, but I'm tired of being anonymous. I want people to know who I am."

"And what makes you so sure that Dedmann was this so-called Third Wise Man? Yes, he was the right age, and God knows he liked his little secrets. But a spy? Sorry, but I just don't see it. I knew him for almost thirty years."

"Maybe you'll believe it after you hear my story. About a year ago, I was helping my grandmother clean out her basement in Brooklyn and found these. The name and address are missing, but when I compared them with the official drawings on file in the buildings department, there's no doubt about it: these are secret blueprints for this house. You see, Marcus, my grandfather

built this house for Dedmann in 1943. These show something that I believe no one else has ever seen—the actual
dimensions of the cellar, including all the nooks and crannies, and tunnels that extend in all directions from the
footprint of the actual house. Come on, Marcus, admit it.
You had no idea there was so much hidden below ground
level."

"Perhaps, but so much the better for all of us. More
rooms, more wine. Secret blueprints, huh? Do you mind
if I take a closer look? These may be helpful. I'll get
them back to you tomorrow."

"That's fine, if it will help convince you. But let me
finish my story. The whole time my grandfather worked
here, he hardly said a word about the house to my grandmother. When she asked why it was taking so long, she
remembers him saying something strange about the cellar. He said it was like the guy was building a clock with
the gears and springs and hundreds of little parts, all of
which were being custom-made by Dedmann. And nobody but Dedmann and my grandfather were allowed
down here while it was under construction. The two of
them built all this.

"And then, two days after he puts the finishing
touches on this house, my grandfather dies. He had
never been sick a day in his life; he didn't smoke, and
barely drank. But that day, he drank some wine that
Dedmann had given him as a parting gift. He poured
himself a glass and sat down in his favorite chair. An

hour later, my grandmother found him—dead. A heart attack, everyone said, and no one even looked at the bottle of wine. Grandma poured the rest of it down the drain, and that was that."

"What are you saying—that Dedmann murdered your grandfather? Ridiculous."

"Shhh! Maybe. Maybe not. How would you explain this? You see this phone number, KL5-4500, and the word 'diary' with the question mark after it, written here in the margin? I did a little digging, and do you know whose number that was? Vernon Ryerson."

"Am I supposed to know who that is?" Klinger snipes.

"You would if you knew anything about the case of the Third Wise Man. Vernon Ryerson was the FBI agent who worked on the case for more than thirty years. He died in 1988, but I did get a look at the case file. I told them I was writing a book about German spies in World War II, so they showed me everything that Ryerson had. I checked his notes; there's no record of a call from my grandfather. I'm willing to bet that Dedmann figured out that my grandfather suspected something, and dealt with him before he had a chance to take action. I can't prove it, though, without more evidence—the kind of evidence that might be stashed here somewhere."

"Was there anything in the file about Dedmann?" Klinger asks. "Was the FBI watching him?"

"Not that I could find," says Lindsay. "But I did a little more snooping, with the help of a private investigator.

He found something very interesting: before 1944, there is only one mention of someone named Curtis Dedmann in the United States, and that Curtis Dedmann died as an infant in northern Maine during the flu epidemic of 1918. Starting in 1944, however, his name starts popping up all over the place. I think that our friend Curtis 'borrowed' his name and birth certificate, and whatever else he needed, from the town hall in Naniscot, Maine. And that, for me, was the 'smoking gun.' "

"Oh? And why is that?"

"Because Naniscot is less than five miles from the spot where a German submarine dropped off three spies in 1942."

"I see," says Klinger. "That might explain some-thing . . . something I've been wondering about." He pauses, and I hear him take a breath and exhale loudly. "What I'm about to tell you stays in this room. Agreed?"

"Agreed."

Klinger continues in a lower voice. "There's another will. A few days before he died, Curtis told me about it. He was going to leave everything—*everything*—to Shel-ley Gallivan."

"What!" cries Lindsay. "Why?"

In the elevator, Margaret and I gasp and then imme-diately cover our mouths.

"The why isn't so important. It's the where that con-cerns me. No one must ever learn about that will."

"Do you know where it is?"

"Yes, I do. It's in the bottom of my fireplace, in ashes. Why do you think I bought nearly everything at the auction? I'd been in touch with Curtis's lawyer, Applewood, and it was obvious he knew nothing about it. Curtis must have done it all on his own, but he never delivered a copy to Applewood. Lucky for us, one of the drawers in that writing desk I bought at the auction had a false bottom, and I found it there."

"So we're safe, then?"

"Sadly, no. Curtis Dedmann must have been the last person alive to use a typewriter and carbon paper, because the version I burned was definitely a carbon copy. The original must still be somewhere in this house."

After Klinger and Lindsay leave the basement, Margaret waits a few minutes before pushing the button to send us back upstairs. I have to shield my eyes from the bright lights of the kitchen as the elevator door opens. Margaret and I take deep breaths, relieved to be able to bend our knees and make a little noise again.

"I was so nervous," says Shelley. "What if that old thing got stuck? Or what if Mr. Klinger opened the door down there and found you? What would he do?"

"It's hard to believe we were only in there for twenty minutes," I say. "It seemed like hours."

"Boy, was it worth it, though," says Margaret. "You won't believe what we heard. We'll tell you the whole story later, but here's the short version: according to Klinger, Mr. Dedmann wrote a new will, and he left everything to you."

"To me? That's crazy! All this . . . this house? Why?"

"I was hoping you could tell us," says Margaret. "But none of that will matter if we don't find the will. Klinger found—and burned—one copy in that desk he bought, but he's positive that there's another. That's why he bought everything at the auction: he was looking for it."

"But . . . what about Mr. Applewood? Wouldn't he have a copy?"

"Not if Dedmann never got around to delivering it," I say. "Remember what he wrote in that notebook? 'Will to GA,' and then that list of three things. Well, my dad helped us figure out that those were wines. But now the first part makes sense: he was sending his will to GA— Garrison Applewood. But, apparently, he died before he got around to delivering it. Klinger seems pretty sure that the lawyer doesn't know anything about it."

Shelley looks genuinely bewildered by this strange turn of events. "I think I've been through everything in the house. I don't know where else to look."

"Check it all again," I say.

"And in the meantime," says Margaret, "promise that you won't let anyone you don't know and trust completely in this house. And don't remove anything else; we just have to hope that the will is still here . . . someplace."

Even though she's only twelve, Margaret has this way of making people trust her, and Shelley accepts what she says without batting an eye.

"Right. No one in. Nothing out. Got it."

"Perfect," says Margaret, handing her a Red Blazer Girls Detective Agency card. "Send me an email if you find anything. If we all play our cards right, your life is going to change in a big way."

Chapter 15

Okay, Rat Number Three— take one step forward and turn to the left

While Margaret and I are waiting to cross Third Avenue on our way home, I realize that I haven't turned my phone on since our claustrophobic eavesdropping session in Dedmann's dumbwaiter. I missed three calls and a text message from Raf, who probably thinks I'm still mad at him about that Coffeeteria incident.

"Hey, he's on this side of town," I say. "Huh. I wonder what he's doing over here."

"You know, you could call him back and find out," Margaret suggests. "I just hope he didn't borrow his uncle's motor scooter again."

"No kidding. If his mom catches him, he'll be grounded for life. He's still paying for the last time," I say as I press the call button.

"It's about time!" Raf scolds. "What are you doing? Where are you?"

"I'm with Margaret, on my way home."

"I'll meet you at Eighty-First and Third. Let's go to a movie."

I put my hand over the phone and turn to Margaret. "You feel like going to a movie?"

"No, I've got too much to do at home. I want to find out a little more about Vermeer and the *View of Delft,* and then we have to figure out when we're going back to Dedmann's house. But you should go—you don't get to see him that much, especially now that Perkatory is closed."

"You're sure?"

"Positive."

I uncover the phone. "Okay. What are we going to see?"

"Rear Window," says Raf. "Alfred Hitchcock, 1954. Jimmy Stewart and Grace Kelly. It's number forty-two on the AFI list."

Raf keeps the American Film Institute's list of the greatest movies of all time in his wallet, checking them off as he sees them. He's not trying to watch them in order or anything like that (which drives Margaret crazy—she would have started with number one hundred and worked her way up to number one), and he tries to see them at theaters whenever possible.

Rear Window is playing on the Hunter College campus, down by St. Veronica's, and when it's over, I have only one question for Raf: "How can a movie that good be only number forty-two on your list? It was amazing."

He grins at me, shaking his head. "You say that every time."

"Well, I still can't believe that *Casablanca* got beat out by *Citizen Kane*. It's no contest."

"You just like Humphrey Bogart when he says, 'Here's looking at you, kid.'"

"Remember that first time you imitated him for Malcolm?"

"Oh, right—Sam Spade, in *The Maltese Falcon*." He lowers his voice an octave or two. "It's the stuff dreams are made of, sweetheart."

Wait a second. Did Raf just call me sweetheart? Or was it part of his Bogart impression? And why am I blushing? Stop it!

"Hey, d'you want to get something to eat?" I ask, changing to a safer subject than romantic movies. "What I really want is a hot chocolate from Perkatory, but I guess I can't have that."

"I thought you said that the stuff from Coffeeteria was pretty good. We could go there. It's close, at least."

Actually, I'm pretty sure I described their hot chocolate as spectacular, but it still doesn't make me want to hand over my money to those destroyers-of-Perkatory-and-all-that-is-good.

But then the bulbs start flashing in my overworked brain: I have an idea. "Fine, let's go to Coffeeteria."

"Really?"

"Sure."

"Should I be afraid?"

I nod gravely. "Very. But, first, we need to buy a jar of peanut butter."

"It's a plan worthy of your friend Alfred Hitchcock," I say after we take our seats at a table and cautiously sip our steaming hot chocolates. "There's going to be a rat-napping, and you're going to help."

"A ratnapping?"

"Uh-huh."

"But . . . why? What good is that going to do?"

"Here's what I think happened: This guy Jeff, who keeps the pet rat in his pocket, discovered when the health inspector was going to be at Perkatory—it can't be that hard to find out stuff like that—and goes over there a little ahead of time and lets his furry friend loose. He probably trained him to go into the kitchen and wait until he called."

"You actually believe that?" says Raf, trying not to laugh. "Using a pet rat to sabotage a rival coffee shop. How can you be sure it's the same rat? You know, I like Perkatory and all, but let's face it, it's not exactly the cleanest place. Maybe it was a real rat. A wild one, I mean. A real New York rat."

"I already thought of that. We'll get the inspector to identify him. It'll be just like on *Law & Order*. A rat lineup."

Raf drops his forehead onto the table. "Sophie. What.

Are. You. Talking. About? A rat lineup? With a New York City health inspector. You're insane."

"Okay, so maybe not the rat lineup. But it doesn't matter—I have a better idea, anyway. Let's just grab the rat and get out of here."

"Just like that?" says Raf, snapping his fingers.

"I've been watching the manager since we got here." I point at a row of coat hooks on the back wall. "You see that dark gray coat, the one with the hood? He goes over to it every few minutes and drops something into the left pocket. Next time he goes into the back room, I'm going to smear some peanut butter on the palm of my glove, grab that little rodent, and stick him in my coat pocket."

"And then what?"

"And then I'm gonna run like crazy."

"I can't believe you're going to do this."

"Says the boy who talked me into riding all over New York on his uncle's scooter."

"I made you wear a helmet."

"Still. There! Did you see that? The manager just dropped something in the pocket. Get ready." I use a coffee stirrer to spread some peanut butter on my left glove. "That ought to keep him busy for a while."

When Jeff opens the door to the kitchen, I make a mad dash for his coat. I glance around the room, making sure no one's watching. Using my non–peanut buttered hand to lift the flap, I peek into the pocket, where an adorable whiskered face peers up at me.

"Why, hello there, Mr. Rat. You want some nice peanut butter? Of course you do."

Naturally, he can't resist the temptation, and clambers up and out of Jeff's pocket and into mine, where I've stuck my glove. And then I turn and walk away, cool as a cucumber.

I did it!

Raf, who looks nervous, waits for me on the sidewalk and hustles me away.

"Did you get him?"

"Of course."

"And you didn't get caught. It's a miracle. You always get caught."

"Oh my gosh, that's right! I didn't get caught!"

"You're a successful criminal . . . with a pet rat."

Chapter 16

In which we look deep into Vermeer's eyes

"You did *what*?" Margaret howls.

"I took matters into my own hands, with the help of a little peanut butter. Well, matters and a rat, if you want to get technical."

"Where are you keeping it? Do you know anything about taking care of a rat?"

"What's to know? It's a rat, Margaret, not a koala bear. He's in my old aquarium. But don't tell my parents. They would freak out. Dad has this thing about rodents."

"Because he's a chef, and rats are disgusting. Did Raf talk you into this?"

"No! He had nothing to do with it, I swear. He thinks I'm crazy."

"He's right. Now that you have this rat, what are you going to do with it?"

"That's what I'm working on. How does this sound to you? 'We have your rat. If you want him back, tell the

160

health department how you set him loose in Perkatory. You'll get him back when they reopen.'"

"I think it sounds like my best friend has lost her mind. A ransom note? Let me guess—you used cutout letters from a magazine, didn't you?"

"Not yet, but I'm going to. This is just a first draft."

"Mr. Eliot would be so proud."

"Hey, do you think he'd give me extra credit?"

"No, I think he would have you arrested."

"Oh. Right. So, did you hear anything from Shelley? She find anything?"

"Nothing yet, but she says she's still looking. We're going by there tomorrow right after school. Don't forget your camera; we might need it. And, Sophie?"

"Yeah?"

"Leave the rat at home."

With the shortest day of the year just around the corner, it is already dark when we sneak past Sturm & Drang and GW Antiques and Curiosities on our way to see Shelley. The lights are on in both places, and each gives off a golden glow, making them look like the warm, inviting places a used-book store and an antiques shop should be. Above both shops, Christmas lights strung around the railings of fire escapes add a unique–to–New York flavor to the neighborhood.

At Curtis Dedmann's house, the white lights of a Christmas tree glow behind the front windows and a beautiful wreath hangs on the door. Shelley and Bertie greet us enthusiastically in the foyer, and then we all rush into the kitchen to demonstrate the dumbwaiter to Leigh Ann and Becca, who have been dying to see it.

"You two can go," I say. "I've had enough of that thing."

"I'm with Sophie on that one," says Margaret. "Meet you downstairs. We'll be waiting for you."

We take the stairs, and sure enough, we get to the basement ahead of the dumbwaiter.

"I think we're stuck," says Leigh Ann. "We stopped moving."

"You're not stuck. Just push on the door," I say, my ear pressed against the wood panel that is the dumbwaiter door.

Becca grunts. "Nothing is— Hey, you're right!"

"Welcome, again," says Shelley.

"All right, let's get to work," says Margaret. "Vermeer is . . . over here." We gather around her as she begins the thorough examination of the medallion.

"Heard anything from Klinger lately?" I ask Shelley. "Or Lindsay?"

"Not a peep. I expect Mr. Klinger is gloating; he's certain that he has 'won' this little battle over the house. And he's probably right. I've looked everywhere, and that will just isn't here."

Leigh Ann pats Shelley on the back. "Don't give up yet."

"That's right," I say. "We still have time." I point at Margaret. "She really is a genius, you know. This Dedmann guy may have been, too, but I'd put her up against anybody in a battle of brainpower."

"Easy, Sophie," says Margaret. "I haven't solved it— Hey . . . ohhhhhh."

"See what I mean?" I say, nudging Shelley.

Margaret looks over her shoulder at the rest of us and waggles her eyebrows. "By George, I think I'm onto something. Watch what happens when I turn this."

She grasps the medallion and spins it clockwise a few degrees. There is a noticeable click as something happens inside the metal disk, revealing a pinprick of light coming from behind the wall, through Vermeer's left eye. When Margaret turns the medallion to the left, the hole closes and the light disappears.

"Cool," says Becca.

Margaret continues wiggling, pushing, pulling, tapping, and turning until she is satisfied that there are no more secrets. She turns the light back on and tries to look through the pinhole to see what's behind.

"The hole is too small," she says. "And the light is too bright. I can't see anything."

"There must be some way to open this section," I say, running my fingers over the panel and the wood trim. "Maybe another one of the medallions."

While I try to get my pathetic, chewed-to-the-nubs

fingernails under the molding, Leigh Ann puts her eye up to the light to see for herself if anything is visible.

As she pulls her head back, Becca shouts, "Wait! Don't move!"

Leigh Ann freezes. "What is it? Is there a spider on me? Get it off!"

"It's not a spider," says Becca. "For once, I swear I'm serious." She pushes the still-terrified Leigh Ann's face closer to the wall and then pulls it back away. "It's the light coming from this hole." Smiling mysteriously, she adds, "Oh, this is good."

"What's good?" I ask.

"The *View of Delft* was revealed to him . . . with a little help," says Becca. "Remember, I was telling you how perfect the perspective is in the painting? Well, there's a reason. When I was at the museum yesterday, I read something about Vermeer. Supposedly, he used this thing called a camera obscura to lay out the perspective." When she sees the confused look on our faces, she continues. "It works kind of like a pinhole camera. The image he wanted to paint was projected on the canvas, and he traced the outlines."

"He cheated?" I say.

"It's not like it was a paint-by-number," Becca replies. "He still had to do the actual painting."

"Oh my gosh," says Margaret, consulting her notebook and reading the second clue aloud: " 'As the view of Delft was revealed to him, shall his eyes to you in a chamber dim, divulge her name and the final quest.' I get it! You're right, Rebecca. Vermeer's eye will reveal the name and the final quest . . . in a chamber dim. Dim . . . dark! That's it! Turn off the lights!"

Flustered, Shelley runs to the bottom of the stairs and flips the switches, plunging the basement—except for Leigh Ann's face—into total darkness.

"Wait!" shouts Margaret. "Turn them back on. We need something flat."

Becca giggles. "How about Sophie's chest?"

"Hey! Not funny," I say.

"Like a piece of poster board," says Margaret. "It needs to be white."

Becca's mouth starts to open: she is grinning like a demon.

"Don't say it, Becca," I warn.

"I have one of those posters from the auction upstairs," says Shelley. "The back is plain white. Will that work?"

Margaret nods. "Perfect."

Shelley runs upstairs and returns with the poster in seconds; she's as excited as the rest of us to see what Margaret has discovered.

Margaret holds the poster about a foot away from the hole in the wall. "Sophie and Becca, you two hold it just like this," she orders. "Now, Shelley, turn the lights off again. Please."

As the lights in the room go out, an illuminated circle appears on the paper between Becca and me.

"Whoa," says Becca. "It's like a projector. . . . Hey, there's something there."

"Start moving the paper away from the wall . . . slowly!" says Margaret. "Stop. Back up an inch. Perfect."

"It's writing," Leigh Ann says, "but it's upside down."

"I don't understand," admits Shelley. "What is going on? Is that a projector?"

"Sort of," answers Margaret. "Did you ever use a pinhole camera?"

"Sure, when I was a kid. My dad helped me make one."

"Well, that's essentially what this is," says Margaret. "Just a slightly bigger version. The image must be on the back wall of the compartment, and when you turn the light on, it projects it through the pinhole. So simple. The answer is revealed to us, just like the *View of Delft* was for Vermeer."

"What does it say?" Shelley asks.

Margaret takes a pen from her pocket and carefully traces the letters. "Okay, that's it. Let's turn the lights back on."

Becca "translates" the upside-down printing:

> Dance with delight and turn your Muse,
> against the clock, no time to lose.
> Beneath the signs, look to the stars,
> which long have held an old man's past,
> in plain sight but unseen for years.

The source, to be revealed at last,
of this not-so-wise man's tears,
by one who looks with eyes like Mars.

"But . . . isn't it supposed to tell us who the Muse is?" I ask. "Wasn't that the whole point?"

Margaret scrunches up her face as she stares at the message. "Um . . . yes . . . I thought so, anyway."

"You guys aren't going to believe this, but I totally know who it is," gushes Leigh Ann. "It just has to be Terpsichore."

"Who?" Becca asks. "Turpentine?"

"Terpsichore," Leigh Ann repeats.

I check out the floor medallions of the nine Muses, and there she is, in one of the corner positions. "How are you so sure it's her? Why not . . . Euterpe? Or Pol-y-hym-ni-a?"

"Because Terpsichore is the Muse of dancers. My teacher talks about her all the time. In fact, technically, dancers are called terpsichoreans. It's kind of strange, though, because I've never seen a picture of her actually dancing. She's always sitting down playing one of those miniature harp things. I forget what it's called."

"Ohhh, I remember her," says Margaret. "You're right. It's a lyre, but it does look a little like a harp. I think she's also the mother of the Sirens, those women in *The Odyssey* who sing the beautiful song and lure sailors to their death."

"What about the second line?" I ask. "What does that mean?"

Margaret glances at the poem. "'Against the clock' . . . It sounds like we have to hurry. Like it's a race against the clock."

Leigh Ann shakes her head. "Or maybe it means to turn her medallion counterclockwise. You know, against the clock."

Margaret claps her forehead with the palm of her hand. "Duh! Of course! Leigh Ann, you're brilliant!"

Leigh Ann's face lights up. "You mean I'm really right?"

"I guess we'll find out when we try to open the lock."

Becca slaps Leigh Ann on the back. "Very nice job, Jaimes. I knew you had it in you. Even if you are from Queens."

"Gee, thanks," Leigh Ann says.

Margaret turns to Shelley. "That's two out of three. Julius Caesar and Terpsichore. One more, and we can open this crazy lock . . . and find out what Mr. Dedmann was hiding."

"I'll keep my fingers crossed," says Shelley. "And if you girls will excuse me, I need to make a call. I'll be right back."

"Wait a second," says Becca as Shelley disappears up the stairs. "We have the first two, right? Caesar and Terpsidancer. Can't we just do those two and then try all the planets, one by one? There's only nine."

"Actually, eight," says Margaret. "Pluto's not considered a true planet anymore. I guess it still was when he put the floor in, though."

"Who cares about Pluto? What about my idea?" Becca asks.

"Nice try," Margaret says, "but it won't work. We can't turn any of the medallions until we get that walking stick. Remember? It's the key."

"Duh!" says Becca. "Forgot about that."

"It's getting late, so let's get to work on the third clue," I say.

Leigh Ann reads the next lines of the poem aloud:

Beneath the signs, look to the stars,
which long have held an old man's past,
in plain sight but unseen for years.

"So, I think we can assume that the old man in the poem is Dedmann," says Margaret. "His past is hidden somewhere in plain sight."

"Beneath the signs," I add. "What's that supposed to mean?"

Margaret taps me on the shoulder and points at the ceiling, where the twelve constellations of the zodiac, made up of gold-leaf stars, glitter between the planets.

"Ohhh. I get it. Capricorn. Aquarius. Gemini. The signs of the zodiac."

"So, if it's beneath the signs, it must be hidden in the floor," Becca deduces.

Margaret says nothing, but moves to the round table, where she stands, bent over the glossy surface of the Milky Way galaxy. A smile creeps across her face as she turns back to us.

"Look to the stars," she says. "The answer is in the stars. This table . . . The Milky Way has something to do with it. I know it."

I look at Becca and Leigh Ann as my arms break out in blueberry-size goose bumps. "Did she just say what I think she said?"

"The answer is in the stars," says Becca. "Just like Madame Zurandot said. Man, that is faa-reaky."

Margaret? Well, let's say she is unimpressed.

"You guys are the biggest suckers. Do you know how many people—this very second—are saying something like 'The answer is in the stars'? Thousands. Millions, probably, if you count other languages. It doesn't mean anything. It's a coincidence, that's all. Now get over here and check this table out . . . every square inch of it."

"Don't forget the last line," Leigh Ann says before crawling underneath the table. "About looking with eyes like Mars. Wasn't he the god of war? What was special about his eyes?"

"Nothing that I can remember," I say. "But you never know with mythology. There are so many stories that it's impossible to keep them all straight. I'll volunteer to do some research."

"And I need to learn more about the Milky Way," says Margaret.

"It looks like a satellite picture of a hurricane," says Becca. "There's the eye, and then these big swirls." She leans over until her face is almost against the polished surface. "I wonder how long it took somebody to do this. It's amazing. There are thousands of stars. They must have used a toothpick to make each one."

"And the colors are right, too," Margaret adds. "White, yellow, blue, orange, and red . . . Those are the colors of stars."

"Any luck?" Shelley asks, returning from upstairs.

"Not yet," says Margaret. "But we're working on it."

"Well, I hate to interrupt your progress, but I have to run across town to see my grandmother. I wouldn't do it now, with all this going on, but it's her birthday, and—"

"It's okay," says Margaret. "Sophie, you remembered your camera, right?"

"Yes, ma'am. Charged and ready." I take it from my backpack and wipe it clean. "What do you want a picture of?"

"I want some close-ups of the tabletop, different sections. Get nice and close so we can see individual stars."

I move around the table, snapping away, and then, with Shelley looking on nervously, I climb on top so I can position myself directly over the center of the galaxy. When I finish there, I hop off the table and wander down the center of the room, taking pictures of the ceiling.

"Just in case," I say.

Chapter 17

Okay, okay, so it wasn't the greatest plan ever conceived

It's just Mom and me for dinner, so we decide to make it a soup and salad night. I make the salad Dad taught me—a true bistro salad, he calls it, with escarole and walnuts and Gruyère cheese. Easy, and infinitely yummy, if I do say so myself. Meanwhile, Mom throws together one of her specialities, this rich, creamy, mushroom soup that she makes using three different kinds of mushrooms. Confession time: I used to hate mushrooms until I tasted this soup. Now I beg her to make it for me at least once a month.

Margaret calls just as I'm slurping up the last bit from my bowl. There's a family rule in the St. Pierre home: we don't answer the phone at dinnertime. You have to remember, the French have a different relationship with food than most people. To my dad, having a phone ring during dinner is like hearing one in church, or the theater.

"Oops, sorry, Mom," I say. "Forgot to turn it off. Oh, it's Margaret."

"That's okay, you can take it," she says. "It's an easy cleanup. Go."

I half expect Margaret to tell me she has solved the third clue, but she hasn't even focused her brainpower on that problem yet, I learn.

"We have a bigger problem," she says. "It's that darn walking stick. I guess it was wishful thinking, but I was just going along, figuring that if we had the combination . . . well, we could basically use anything to spin the center of those three medallions. But I took a closer look today, and now I'm positive: we have to have Dedmann's walking stick; there's no two ways about it. It really does work like a key."

"What do you mean?"

"Well, those holes in the center of the medallions are a lot more complicated than I thought. Inside each one there are a bunch of different-shaped . . . buttons, I guess you'd call them, sticking out. Some of them are solid, but some of them move. They push in so they're perfectly flush with the rest of the socket."

"Wait, I'm confused."

"Don't worry, I'll show you what I mean the next time we're in there. But we need that walking stick. Otherwise, it's like trying to jam the wrong key into a lock. Unless it drops in perfectly and pushes in all the right buttons, we won't be able to turn it. You see what I mean?"

"Sort of. I believe you, though. So how do we get the stick?" I know what Margaret is going to say the moment those words leave my lips.

"I have a plan."

I smile to myself. Do I know my best friend or what?

"You always do," I say.

Dad gets home really late from the restaurant, but he leaves a killer gift for me on the kitchen table: a box of six *pains au chocolat*. I do a happy dance around the kitchen as I wolf one down. And then there were five.

Margaret's eyes widen when I meet her in the lobby; she recognizes the box immediately. "Croissants?"

"Avec chocolat."

"Mmm. *Très bien.*"

And then there were four. Oops. Make that three; once I open the box, I can't avoid helping myself to another.

"That was amazing," she says, her eyes glued to the box.

"I have to save two for Becca and Leigh Ann," I say. "Don't I?"

"Well, we could eat the rest. If they don't know they missed them, they can't really miss them, right?"

"Kind of like, if a *pain au chocolat* falls in the forest, and no one is there to eat it, did it really taste good, anyway?"

"Exactly!"

I start to open the box, but something stops me. "No. We can't. We have to share. It's the Red Blazer way."

Margaret nods sadly. "You're right. Listen to us. And a week before Christmas. Like a couple of Scrooges."

We meet Becca and Leigh Ann in the cafeteria before school and I set the box on the table between them.

And then there was one.

"Hey, guys, what's going on?" says Livvy Klack, appearing at my side. "Ooh. What's that?"

"Um, it's yours," I say.

"Really? Thanks! Hey, did you hear about Perkatory? They're going to reopen on Saturday night."

"Yay!" we shout, earning ourselves a scowl from Sister Eugenia, who is passing by.

"I know, right?" says Livvy, tearing off an enormous chunk of *pain* with her teeth. "It's about time. I never realized how long I spent in there until it was gone. The only good thing is that I think I lost two pounds. Thank God they don't sell these. I would weigh a ton."

"How did you hear about Perk?" I ask.

"I was in that new place, Coffeeteria, waiting at the counter for my coffee, and I heard a couple of people talking about it, and then I went by this morning and there was a sign on the door."

Margaret eyes me suspiciously. "Did you ever . . . ?"

"No. I never had a chance," I say. "I was going to do it yesterday, but after school we were in such a hurry to get uptown to Shelley's that I forgot."

"What are you two whispering about?" Leigh Ann asks.

"You won't believe what Sophie did," Margaret says. "You know the manager over at Coffeeteria, Jeff? She kidnapped his pet rat."

"What?" cries Livvy.

"Nice," says Becca. "Well played, St. Pierre."

Leigh Ann shudders. "A rat?" She backs away from me. "You don't have him with you now, do you?"

"No, he's home in an aquarium," I say. "In my closet. Now what am I supposed to do?"

Livvy holds up a hand. "Wait. Why did you take his rat? Just for spite?"

"Oh no," says Margaret. "This is Sophie St. Pierre, the girl with the world's most vivid imagination. She actually thought that the manager at Coffeeteria had planted his rat in Perkatory at the exact time the health inspector would be there so they would get shut down. The best part, though, was her ransom note: 'We have your rat.' And then telling him he has to make things right with Perkatory if he wants the rat back alive."

"No. Way," says Leigh Ann.

"Oh, totally way," Margaret replies. "But she never delivered the ransom note, and now Perkatory is reopening."

"You really are crazy, aren't you?" Livvy asks. "I love it! A ratnapping!"

"There! See!" I shout. "Somebody gets it. It still could have been him. Just because I didn't send the note—"

"What are you going to do now?" Becca asks. "You gonna kill the rat?"

"What? No! Of course not!"

"You want me to take care of it? Because I, uh, know people."

"Nobody is going to whack the rat. He's innocent. I just have to slip him back into the guy's coat pocket. I got him out; I can get him back in . . . and in one piece, Becca."

While Leigh Ann and Livvy rehearse their scenes in *The Merry Gentlemen,* Becca sketches like mad, and Margaret checks and rechecks her math homework, I do something I've never done in school: I take a little nap. Even in kindergarten, when it was encouraged (or forced on me, depending on how you look at it), I refused to do it. I was convinced that I would miss something important. It's hard to imagine now just what that something might have been, but at the time, it was life-or-death stuff.

Maybe it was those two pastries I had for breakfast, or maybe staying awake until eleven-thirty to finish the first book in the series that Becca swears is "almost as good as *The Lord of the Rings*" is the problem. Either way, I put my head down on a desk—I've seen lots of other kids do it—and in seconds, I'm out cold . . . and dreaming I'm in France again.

As usual in these dreams, I'm on the back of a scooter with my arms wrapped around Raf's waist—*ooh la la*. We're zooming down a country lane with vineyards on both sides, and then slow down as we approach a small village. There's an old church on the left, and a bride and groom are standing at the door waving at us. Raf pulls up in front, and that's when it gets weird. First, I realize that I know the two people: it's my aunt Noëlle—my dad's sister, who lives in a town that looks a lot like the one in my dream—and her husband, Christian. There's another woman standing a few steps below them—a woman I've seen before, but only in my dreams—smiling sweetly directly at me.

"*Bonjour,* Sophie," she says. "*Et joyeux Noël.* The stars are full of secrets. Look to the stars." And then—poof!—she's gone.

"The stars?"

My eyes turn back to the happy couple, but something very, very strange has happened. That's not Uncle Christian standing there in that tux—it's Raf. The bride, however, has turned away so I can't see her face.

"Turn around," I say. "Please."

"Sophie," someone calls.

"Raf!" I shout.

"Sophie!"

I jerk awake and find myself surrounded by an army

of red blazers, plaid skirts, and laughing faces. The look on my face must be one of absolute confusion, because it makes them all laugh even harder.

"Jeez, St. Pierre," says Becca. "Where were you?"

I find Margaret's face in the crowd. "You were talking in your sleep," she says. "You said something about stars, and then told someone to turn around—"

"And then you shouted Raf's name," says Leigh Ann. "It was adorable."

"France again?" Margaret asks. "The scooter?"

I nod. "It was outside a church in some little village, and my aunt and uncle were—" I stop as the answer to the third clue rumbles into my brain like the M15 bus running a red light. I leap to my feet. "We have to go. Now." I race to the locker I share with Margaret and grab my coat.

"What's the matter?" Margaret says as she pins me against the locker next to ours. "I haven't seen you move that fast since that time Raf called Leigh Ann, and you thought they were going out. What happened in that dream?"

"I can't tell you. Not all of it, anyway. But that's not it. I . . . remembered something. Something important. I have to go home and get it, and then I'll meet you guys at Dedmann's house. Trust me, okay?"

"What are you up to?"

"Eyes like Mars," I say. "I know what he means."

Margaret releases my coat but continues to stare at

me suspiciously. "Okay, but if you're not there in half an hour, we're coming after you. Right, everybody?"

Becca and Leigh Ann nod their agreement while Livvy looks on.

Margaret hesitates a second before turning to Livvy. "Do you want to come, too?" Margaret asks. "We can fill you in on what we've been doing on the way up there."

Wow.

Even though I'm in a huge hurry, I have to stop to let that sink in. Margaret and Livvy don't exactly . . . Well, let's just say that those two are kind of like England and France—at war for centuries, but now they're allies. Sort of.

Even though Livvy played a big part in our last case, she's still in the "honorary" category of Red Blazer Girls, along with Elizabeth Harriman and Malcolm Chance (whose blazer would have to be red tweed). So for Margaret to actively invite Livvy to join us is a pretty big deal.

Livvy's eyebrows move a few degrees north in surprise, but her whole face lights up. "Really? Yes! The way you've all been acting, I knew you were up to something."

"Oh, we're up to something, all right," says Margaret, staring directly at me. "Some of us more than others."

Chapter 18

In which Madame Zurandot starts to look pretty darn clever

The streetlights are already on, and everyone else is inside when I arrive, panting, at Dedmann's house. I check my watch: twenty-eight minutes.

Bertie is first to say hello, the entire back half of her body wagging crazily.

"Why didn't I get a greeting like that?" Becca asks.

"Because I'm her favorite," I say, dropping to the floor to be covered in dog kisses. "Dogs know who their real friends are."

"Boy, she really does like you," Shelley says. "Maybe you should just take her home with you today. But first, the girls tell me that you think you know how to solve the third clue, but that you're being very secretive about it. Shall we go to the cellar?"

We follow her down the stairs and to the round table, where everyone sits and waits for me to start talking.

"This had better be good," Becca says. "Or I'm never

going to let you forget that little sleep-talking episode we just witnessed."

"Like you were going to, anyway," I say.

"Ohhh, Raaafff," she says, swooning.

"Come on, Becca," scolds Leigh Ann. "Let her talk. The suspense is killing me."

I stick my tongue out at Becca. "Thank you, Leigh Ann. Okay, remember that I told you my aunt and uncle were in my dream? Well, there was somebody else." I point at the Ring of Rocamadour on my right hand. "She was there, too."

Margaret, Becca, and Leigh Ann know exactly who I mean, but Livvy and Shelley share a confused look.

"Ever since we found the ring—the real one—this woman keeps showing up in my dreams, just like in the legend."

"Legend?" Shelley asks.

"Uh-huh. Supposedly, whoever wears the ring receives visits from . . . I know this sounds bizarre . . . St. Veronica. And she makes your wishes come true . . . somehow. I know, crazy, right?"

"What does she look like? I mean, how do you know who she is?" asks Livvy.

"I suppose she looks like what you think she ought to look like," I say. "Usually, she looks just like the painting of her in the church. This time, though, she may have had a little of Madame Zurandot thrown in, too."

"What did she say?" Margaret asks.

"She said 'Hi,' and 'Merry Christmas,' in French. And then she said, 'The stars are full of secrets' and 'Look to the stars.' That was it. Then I woke up."

Leigh Ann looks disappointed. "That's it?"

"Not quite," I say. "Seeing my aunt . . . reminded me of the Christmas card she sent me last year. This card." I take a card from its envelope and set it on the table. "She makes her own cards every year, and they're always, like, wacky-creative. Here, check it out yourselves." I pass it to Margaret, who opens and closes it several times, smiling at the card's "magic," before passing it on to the others.

You see, the inside of the card is an indoor scene of a Christmas tree, decorated with red lights and red ornaments, with packages wrapped in red—very festive-looking. The front fold of the card, however, has a special feature: an oval is cut out, large enough to reveal the picture of the tree inside. But the oval is covered with red cellophane, and when the card is closed, the lights, ornaments, and presents all magically disappear, leaving a simple fir tree.

"This is pretty clever," says Livvy. "The red plastic filters out all the red light, so anything that appears red to our eyes just disappears. I saw something like this once at a planetarium. That's how they can tell what stars and other stuff are made of."

Oh yeah. Whatever you might think about Livvy, she's no dummy.

"Ohhh!" says Margaret. "Look with eyes like Mars! Mars is the red planet. Look with red eyes. Nice work, Sophie."

"And the answer is in the stars," I say. "It's written in the stars. I thought we might need something a little bigger than the Christmas card, so I brought this." I take out a red plastic report cover that is exactly the same color as the cellophane in the card.

I set the report cover on top of the painted Milky Way and watch as all the red stars disappear beneath it. At the same time, with all the red ones gone, the light blue stars seem to pop out from the image.

"Move it right to the center of the galaxy," Margaret says. "There . . . stop. Do you see it?"

We all stand on tiptoe and stretch as far as we can to see what she's pointing out.

"It's writing," says Leigh Ann, taller than I am, and able to get a closer look.

I slide the red plastic rectangle across the tabletop, following one of the swirls of the Milky Way and reading: "I . . . am . . . the . . . Third . . . Wise . . . Man."

"Oh my," says Shelley. "Then it's true. Mr. Dedmann really was a German spy."

"Not just a spy—a famous spy. The Third Wise Man," says Margaret. "This is huge. But we still need more."

"Keep going," Becca says. "There are a lot of stars left to check. Each one of these swirls has hundreds. Thousands."

I try to hand her the card, but she refuses. "No, you keep going. This is your moment of glory."

"It's a little tricky to read," I say.

"Try over here," says Leigh Ann. "This looks like it could be something."

I push the cover toward her fingertips. "Oh, okay, here we go. 'My . . . name . . . was . . . Kaspar . . . Neuner. I . . . had . . . a wife . . . Venus . . . and . . . a son . . . Kaspar.'"

"His wife's name was Venus!" Margaret shouts. "The planet! And remember his poem? The source of this not-so-wise man's tears. He had a family. I wonder what happened to them."

Shelley, so pale that she seems almost transparent, slumps into a chair.

"Are you okay?" I ask. "You look like you saw a ghost."

She smiles weakly up at me. "I think maybe I just did. You see, my mother's maiden name was Neuner. And her grandmother, my great-grandmother . . . you won't believe this . . . was named Venus. That just can't be a coincidence. Which makes Mr. Dedmann, or Kaspar Neuner, whoever he was, my great-grandfather."

"Oh my gosh. That means that the picture he had in his hand when he died—the one with the 'V' on the back—must be Venus," I say to Shelley. "Your great-grandmother."

"His one true love," says Leigh Ann. "So sad. And romantic. After all those years . . ."

"And that's why he changed his will, I'll bet," says Margaret. "He probably just figured out that he had a real heir."

"But . . . why didn't he go back to Germany after the war?" I ask, continuing to search the stars for more information. "Or have his family come here?"

"There are a million possible reasons," Margaret says. "But right now, we have to focus on what we do know. We absolutely have to find that will. Fast."

"Well, we have the three pieces of the puzzle," says Becca. "All we need now is that walking stick."

"I saw Marcus Klinger out on the street earlier today, and he had it with him," Shelley reports. "In fact, I haven't seen him without it in days. I'll bet he keeps the darn thing under his pillow when he sleeps."

The left side of Margaret's mouth curls up in a half smile as the last bank of circuits in that supercomputer she calls a brain are switched on.

"Uh-oh. I know that look," I say.

"Me too," says Leigh Ann. "Margaret Wrobel has a plan."

Chapter 19

In which I come face to face with my old pal Mr. Winterbutt

And, oy, what a plan it is. All we need to pull it off, Margaret informs us, is a container of Play-Doh, some epoxy, and the kidnapped rat (whom I have nicknamed Humphrey). Oh, and a little help from our old friend Gordon Winterbottom. That's all.

"Play-Doh?" I ask.

Margaret nods. "And epoxy."

"Isn't that some kind of glue?" asks Leigh Ann.

"Sort of," says Margaret. "It comes in a pack with two tubes, one of resin, and the other, a hardener. You mix the two parts together, which causes a chemical reaction. When it dries, it's hard as a rock."

"You're going to glue Klinger's shoes to the floor, aren't you?"

Another mysterious smile appears on Margaret's face. "No, but that's not a bad idea. Listen, I promise I'll explain everything, but right now, we need to talk to Mr. Winterbottom. And, Sophie?"

"Yeah?"

"We have to be nice to him."

"Harrumph. I don't know why you think he's going to help us. He hates us, especially me."

"Well, for one thing," Margaret says, "we have a special card up our sleeves: Winnie."

"What about her?" Becca asks.

"We know where she is," I say.

"And anyone can see that those two lovebirds just need a little push in the right direction," Margaret adds. "They're meant to be together."

"Yeah, like a lit match and gasoline," I say.

"Maybe I can put in a good word with Gordon, too," says Shelley. "Remember, he helped me prepare Mr. Dedmann's books and those other items for the auction at Bartleman's, and he made a nice little profit for himself. And who knows, there may be more things to sell . . . if everything works out. You know, ever since you told me about the will, I've been thinking. If Mr. Dedmann, er, Neuner, really did leave me everything, I'm going to turn this old house into a school of the arts for neighborhood kids. Music. Art classes. Dance. Maybe even a science lab. Who knows? Wouldn't that be perfect?"

"Are you serious? That would be amazing," says Margaret.

Shelley nods. "It would, wouldn't it? Yes, I am serious. It's the opportunity of a lifetime."

Shelley has another piece of information that proves helpful: Gordon stops by the same diner on his way home almost every day. It's only two blocks away, so we bundle up and head out into the cold, dark evening.

A melancholy-looking Gordon Winterbottom sits on a stool at the counter, his shoulders sagging lower than usual as he sips a cup of coffee and then violently jabs a fork into a piece of cherry pie.

"Hello, Mr. Winterbottom," says Shelley, approaching first and standing to his right. "Remember me? Shelley Gallivan? You helped me sort out Curtis Dedmann's estate. Do you mind if we join you?"

He spins around, and his eyes grow narrow as he realizes exactly who the "we" is in her question.

"*You* are certainly welcome. But I have nothing to say to these . . . hoodlums. Nothing but trouble," he grumbles.

"Not a good start," I whisper to Leigh Ann.

"You might want to listen to what they have to say," says Shelley. "They've been a big help to me—"

"Help! I'll bet!" he says, glaring right at me. "Criminals, they are. Don't know why you're mixed up with them, Miss Gallivan."

"Well, let me tell you. Thanks to these girls, I just learned that Curtis Dedmann was my great-grandfather, and that he changed his will shortly before he died. He intended to leave his house and everything inside to me. But there's one big problem. Marcus Klinger—"

"—is a damn fool!" Gordon growls.

"I couldn't agree more," says Shelley. "But he has something that we need. He knows about the will; in fact, he's already destroyed one copy of it. We're still trying to locate the original."

"What does he have that's so important?"

"A walking stick. Remember, from the auction?"

"What's so special about this stick?"

"It's kind of a long story," Shelley says. "But if we don't get the stick, Marcus Klinger and the other members of his Beethoven club will inherit the house."

"What does this have to do with me? Why don't you just steal it?" he asks, again focusing on me. "You don't seem to have a problem with stealing, do you?"

Man, he is bitter. And I can't believe he remembered that little blemish on my otherwise flawless record. It's true: when I was in the fourth grade, I stole a St. Christopher medal from the gift shop at St. Patrick's Cathedral and got caught by Sister Antonia, who made me work there every Saturday for months and promise never to steal again—and I haven't. Gordon found out about my dirty little secret when Margaret and I got caught sneaking around St. Veronica's one night, back when he was the church deacon.

Oh, I know what you're thinking: Not so fast, there, Sophie. What about that recent ratnapping incident? Well, I'll tell you, that is a totally different situation. I didn't steal the rat; I just borrowed him for a while, in the name of justice. Yep. That's my story, and I'm sticking to it.

"We're not going to steal it," Margaret says. "And we're not asking you to, either. We just need you to do one little thing for us. It will only take a second."

"Why would I help you?"

Margaret holds up one finger. "One, because although you may be Scrooge on the outside, deep down, you're a good person. Malcolm Chance told us about all the good things you used to do for the church, and for the kids at St. Veronica's, when you were deacon there. He said that you've paid kids' tuition bills—anonymously— when you knew the families couldn't afford to. So, no matter how mad you might be at us, and how many not-so-great things you may have done, you're not all bad. This could be a second chance for you to really prove it to the world."

"What on earth does Marcus Klinger's walking stick have to do with a second chance for me?"

"Well, this is where the story gets interesting," answers Margaret. "Shelley wants to turn Mr. Dedmann's old place into a school for arts and science, and this could be an opportunity for you to help her get it on its feet.

Come on, Mr. Winterbottom—a school for kids who want to study music and art and science. How can that be a bad thing?"

"Think about it like this," I say. "If we're in school, we won't be out on the streets bothering people."

Becca slaps him on the back, much to his surprise. "And who knows, there might even be a position for you. Right, Shelley?"

"How does director of maintenance sound?" Shelley suggests.

Gordon sits up a little straighter on his stool. "I'm still listening."

"Two," Margaret says, holding up a second finger. "Shelley says the attic is full of old furniture that will need to be . . . evaluated, and then sold, to help raise money for the school."

"And I would be happy to give the job to GW Antiques and Curiosities," says Shelley. "To tide you over until the school opens."

Gordon scratches his chin. "Ten percent commission?"

Shelley smiles. "I was thinking fifteen would be more fair to you. There are some big pieces. You're going to have to hire movers."

"So, what do you think, Mr. Winterbottom?" Margaret asks.

Leigh Ann leans close to Margaret. "Hey, aren't you

forget—" She stops when she sees the look in Margaret's eyes.

Gordon stares Margaret down, his eyes unblinking for an unhealthy length of time. "You're quite a salesman. I may have to hire you when all this is said and done."

"Salesperson," says Margaret. "And thank you. That means you'll do it?"

"Well, I still haven't heard what you want me to do, but if it's within reason, and gives me a chance to put one over on that fathead Marcus Klinger, why not?"

As we leave the diner with, of all people, Gordon Winterbottom on our side, Leigh Ann turns to Margaret. "Why didn't you tell him about Winnie?"

"Simple. The fish was already on the hook. I didn't need to give him any more bait."

"The fish? Ohhh. Right. So you're— Wait . . . so we're not going to try to get them back together?"

"I never said that. There's a time for peace, and a time for war. On Thursday, we go to war. Then we worry about Gordon and Winnie."

Before we can go to war, however, we have to prepare, and that means cooking up a homemade batch of Play-Doh and refilling a bottle of 1949 Château Latour. (C'mon, admit it: you are dying to know what that is all about, especially the Play-Doh. Sorry, but for security reasons, I'm authorized to tell you only that it is "part of the plan.")

"I've made it before," says Margaret as everyone invades the kitchen at my apartment after school on Wednesday. She lines up the ingredients on the counter. "Flour, water, salt, oil, and cream of tartar."

"What color is it going to be?" I ask.

Margaret shrugs. "Flour-, water-, and salt-colored, I suppose. Some shade of beige?"

"Beige Play-Doh?" Becca protests. "I'm sorry, Margaret, but as an artist, I can't let you do that. Sophie, do you have any food coloring?"

I climb onto the counter so I can reach the back of the cabinet where Dad hides the little bottles from me. (He still hasn't forgotten the famous "green mashed potato incident.") "Here we go, red and blue. And green! My favorite."

"Guys, what difference does it make?" Margaret asks. "We're not making little animals. Beige is fine. Buuuttt, now that I think of it, we could use some food coloring." She hands me a packet of grape Kool-Aid. "You and Leigh Ann are going to make wine, and you can start by mixing up a big pitcher of this. Then you can add some red and blue until it looks dark enough to be red wine."

While Margaret stirs and Rebecca kneads food coloring into the fake Play-Doh, Leigh Ann and I make a quart of delicious-looking fake wine.

"One more thing," says Margaret, setting the empty bottle from 1949 on the counter. "We need a cork."

"Not a problem," I say. "We have thousands."

"Thousands?" Leigh Ann asks. "Really?"

I shrug. "My dad has been saving them for years."

"Your parents are, like, a lot different from mine," she says, following me to the living room, where I reach into the bottom of a basket and take out a handful of corks.

"We need a nice old one. Maybe with some stains on it. We'll have to stick some glue down in the hole where the corkscrew went—otherwise, it'll leak."

Leigh Ann takes a few more from the basket and examines them. "How about this one?"

She hands me the darkest of the bunch, well stained by wine.

"Perfect," I say. "It's in good shape, but not too good. Now let's see if we can get it into the bottle."

Back in the kitchen, I quickly learn that getting wine and a cork back into a bottle is perhaps a job best left to professionals. Dad has hidden his funnel from me, too (a science experiment gone bad), so I end up splashing purple Kool-Aid all over the kitchen and me. The rest I pour into four glasses.

Becca takes a sip of hers and swishes the fake wine around her mouth like she's seen my dad do a million times. Then she purses her lips and lifts her tiny, un-French nose high in the air.

"A looovely vin-tage," she says. "I taste wet news-paper . . . rotten apples . . . and turpentine. Maybe a touch of day-old chewing gum. Delightful. Delicious. De-contaminated."

And then, of all the kitchens in all the world, Dad chooses this kitchen and this moment to walk into mine. He gasps when he sees the havoc we've wreaked and what seems to be going on. On my left, Becca, her hands stained with splotches of bright green and blue, and with faux wine dribbling down her chin, holds her glass up, about to propose a toast. On my right, Margaret is using all her strength to grip a full bottle of 1949 Château La-tour while Leigh Ann struggles to cram the cork into the neck. Flour and spilled Kool-Aid are everywhere, and on the stovetop sits one of his prized possessions—a huge copper saucepan from the best pot-and-pan-maker in Paris—filled with a sticky, turquoise-ish mess.

"My good saucepan! Sophie! What have you done to my kitchen?"

In these situations, I've learned, play it cool. Non-chalant, even.

"Oh, hey, Dad. *Qu'est-ce que tu fait?*"

A sudden, horrible idea strikes him, and his face clouds over. He considers us—and the contents of his beloved copper pot—carefully, before asking, "*Mon Dieu,* girls. Are you making . . . plastic explosives? In my saucepan?" (I'm not sure which was more upsetting to him: the possibility that we were making explosives, or that we were using his good pan to do it.) "And are you drinking . . . wine?"

"What! No!" I shout. "No to everything you said. Dad, how could you even think that? Like we're terrorists or something. Jeez, we're making our own Play-Doh. And this is Kool-Aid."

He would like to be relieved, I think, but from the completely blank look on his face, he has absolutely no idea what I have just said. "Play . . . dough. Why is it that . . . horrible color? And what does one do with . . . play dough?"

"Silly, one plays with it," I say.

"It's kind of like modeling clay, Mr. St. Pierre," Margaret explains. "It's all-natural. It won't hurt your pan, and we'll clean it up, I promise."

"One more question," he says, pressing a finger into the turquoise blob that has sullied his beloved pan. "Why?"

"Oh, you can use it for lots of things," I say. "You know, school projects, Christmas decorations. That kind of stuff." Vague? Definitely. The truth? Absolutely.

Dad smiles, nodding at my nonanswer. "I see. You're not going to tell me. As long as you're not going to blow something up, I'm happy. One thing I will say: life is never boring when you girls are around."

"Thanks, Dad. That's the nicest thing you've ever said."

But before I let him completely off the hook, let's

tally things up. In the past two weeks, we've been called hooligans (Mr. Eliot), delinquents (Marcus Klinger), hoodlums and criminals (Mr. Winterbottom), and now my own father has basically accused us of being the mad bombers of the Upper East Side.

And we're such sweet girls . . . really!

Dear Reader,

Don't think I haven't noticed that you've been getting a free ride for the past few chapters, while we Red Blazer Girls have been chasing clues all over town in the snow and the cold (and enduring a series of undeserved insults along the way). Well, honey, the party's over: it's your turn—time for you to earn your own red blazer. The heavy lifting has already been done for you: thanks to us, you know the combination to Mr. Dedmann's secret cellar (Julius Caesar, Terpsichore, and Venus). You also know that you need his walking stick, which Marcus Klinger has and is unwilling to part with.

So, what would you do? Can you come up with a plan to open the vaults in the secret cellar without committing a felony or destroying everything in the house? That means you can't steal the walking stick!

At your disposal is an imaginary tote bag with a container of homemade Play-Doh, a bottle of fake 1949

Château Latour, a tube of epoxy, and a kidnapped rat—
exactly the same tools that we have. Your friends (and Mr.
Winterbottom—how scary is that?) await your instructions.

When you think you're ready, turn the page.

Your friend,

Sophie

P.S. Oh, one more thing: have you figured out why
Curtis Dedmann was so obsessed with the number
nine? I have.

P.P.S. I'll be watching.

Chapter 20

You call that a plan! Get back to work!

I don't care what they say about these late-December days being the shortest days of the year; Thursday lasts forever. Most of my classmates have already checked out for Christmas vacation, and now it is official: most of the teachers have joined them.

But not Mr. Eliot.

It is dress rehearsal day for *The Merry Gentlemen*, and every second of his class counts. We scramble to get into costumes and then race down the halls to the stage, where he has everything prepared. Exactly ten minutes after the bell, he opens the curtain, and we are on our way.

And . . . it's not bad. Not great, maybe, but definitely an improvement over the "dreadful" and "shockingly bad" reviews our fearless director had delivered to us following the Monday and Tuesday rehearsals.

"That was nice," says Mr. Eliot. "For a moment there, I forgot that I wrote this mess, and actually started to enjoy myself. Livvy and Leigh Ann—fantastic. Don't change a thing for tomorrow. They're going to love you. And great job, everyone else. Um, Miss St. Pierre, a question: what did you have in your coat pocket when you first came onstage? I could swear I saw something moving."

My hand flies to my pocket in a full-blown panic. "Oh no. No. No. No. Humphrey!"

Margaret, Livvy, and I immediately drop to our knees, crawling around the stage and looking for Humphrey the rat. Leigh Ann? Well, she goes the opposite direction: she climbs onto a table.

"What is going on?" Mr. Eliot demands. "What are you looking for?" When it's clear we're too preoccupied to answer, he turns to Leigh Ann. "Who is Humphrey?"

"You mean *what* is Humphrey? He's a rat," says Leigh Ann. "Sophie kinda, er, borrowed him from some guy. She's been taking care of him for a few days."

A whole gaggle of girls scream, "Rat!" and run to the back of the auditorium, where they stand on the seats.

Mr. Eliot, flabbergasted, slaps his forehead with the palm of his hand so hard that everyone stops to see where the noise came from. "You brought a rat to school, Sophie? Even for you, that's impressive."

"Just help us find him, George. You can yell at me later," I shout from the far corner of the stage.

"Did she really just call me George?" Mr. Eliot asks

Leigh Ann. "What is going on here? Aren't you going to help?"

"Don't look at me," Leigh Ann says from the safety of her tabletop. "I hate rats."

"We have to find this thing before anybody else comes in here," says Mr. Eliot.

From stage left enters our beloved principal, Sister Bernadette, probably wondering why Mr. Eliot's students are screaming.

Unfortunately, I don't notice her unscripted entrance, and that, of course, is the moment I choose to shout, "It's okay, I found him!" and run to downstage center—holding Humphrey high so everyone can see him.

More screaming. Much more screaming.

Sister Bernadette raises her hand for silence and clears her throat. "Miss St. Pierre!"

My mouth is as dry as the Sahara and my tongue suddenly feels like a fat slab of bologna as I ever-so-casually slip poor Humphrey into my pocket. "Y-yes, Sister?"

"Don't you 'yes, Sister' me, young lady," she glowers. "What did you just put in your pocket?"

"Well, it's a, um, a . . . rat. But he's tame! He's a pet! He wouldn't hurt anybody."

"A pet. Rat. Miss St. Pierre, let's talk, shall we? My office!" She spins and starts to walk away.

"No!" says Livvy, stepping forward and standing next to me. "He's mine. It's my fault."

Sister Bernadette stops and turns back to face us, her eyebrows raised.

"What are you doing?" I whisper at Livvy.

"Remember that broken nose?" she asks under her breath. "And all that other mean stuff I did to you? I owe you."

"Are you sure?"

She nods. "It's no big deal."

"Okay," I say, "but if you get into serious trouble, I'm going to tell her the truth."

"Miss Klack?" Sister Bernadette says. "You were saying?"

"I said, he's my rat," says Livvy.

Sister Bernadette moves closer and closer to her, until her face is mere inches from Livvy's. "Humph. We'll see. Meet me in my office." When Livvy is gone, she turns back to me. "I don't know what's going on here, Miss St. Pierre, but I have a feeling that I have not yet reached the bottom of this story." She scowls at my pocket, where Humphrey is snacking on some sunflower seeds. "You have exactly five minutes to get that into a cage of some kind, or I will take care of it the way we usually deal with rodents around here. Do I make myself clear?"

"Yes, Sister!"

With Margaret and Leigh Ann hot on my tail, I run up to the fourth floor and knock on the door of the biology lab, where Ms. Lonneman is enjoying the last few quiet minutes of her free period.

"Oh, thank God," I say when she opens the door. "Ms.LonnemanyouhavetohelpmedoyouhaveacageIcanuseforafewhours?"

"Slow down, Sophie. All I got was something about a . . . cage."

While trying to catch my breath, I take Humphrey from my pocket and hold him up. "Need a cage . . . for . . . the rest of the . . . day . . . for him."

"He's beautiful," she says unexpectedly. She holds out her hands. "Let me see. What's his name?"

"Humphrey," I say, gently passing him over the desk to her.

"*Rattus norvegicus,*" she says, holding him right in front of her face. "About a year old, I'd guess. In college, I worked in the labs with hundreds just like him. Where did you get him?"

"That's, um, kind of a long story," I say. "I'm sort of taking care of him for a few days. But Sister Bernadette found out, and if I don't get him in a cage in the next . . . two minutes . . ."

"I have just the thing," says Ms. Lonneman, retrieving a small hamster cage from the storage room and setting it on her desk. "I don't know if you realize this or not, but your friend Humphrey here is, or was, a lab rat. See, he has these two notches on his ear. Those are for identification."

"What does that mean?" Leigh Ann asks as she cautiously leans in for a closer look. "They did experiments on him? That's terrible."

"It's not always what you think," says Ms. Lonneman. "Lots of them are used in psychology classes, to show how they learn, how they behave in certain—" The bell rings, cutting her off.

"Can we leave him here for now?" I ask. "So I can tell Sister B. that he's, um, safe."

"Sure, he can keep me company this afternoon," she says. "Undoubtedly, he'll be more attentive in class than most of my students."

At lunch, Margaret and I take turns telling Becca the "Humphrey Goes to Dress Rehearsal" story, which has her falling out of her chair laughing.

"It's not funny, Rebecca," says Leigh Ann. "I think Sister Bernadette was serious. I hate to think what she would have done to poor Humphrey if we hadn't found a cage."

"Listen to you," I say. "Suddenly he's poor Humphrey. An hour ago he was just a rat. You hate rats."

"That was before I found out he was an innocent victim."

"Aren't we all?" says Becca earnestly.

Livvy joins us at our table, smiling sheepishly.

"I got a week's detention, but it doesn't start until after vacation," she tells us. "Sister B.'s not even calling my parents. I think she's given up on trying to get in touch with them."

Livvy's parents travel almost constantly for business, and Livvy ends up spending a lot of time with friends and relatives around the city.

"I still can't believe what you did for Sophie," says Margaret admiringly. "That was so . . . brave."

"Yeah, um, thanks," I say. "It *was* pretty nice."

Okay, maybe I'm not going to put Shakespeare out of business, but it was sincere.

And then something completely unexpected happens: Livvy Klack actually blushes. Of course, it's nothing like the classic dunked-in-red-paint look I'm known for, but there is definitely a pinkish glow to her cheeks.

"It was no big deal," she says. "You guys would have done it for me."

Becca, who says pretty much everything that crosses her mind, regards the faces around the table and announces gloomily, "Well, it's official. The world is coming to an end. I mean, if Leigh Ann worrying about a rat and these two becoming friends aren't sure signs, I don't know what is." She shakes my hand. "Been nice knowing you, St. Pierre. See you on the other side."

Chapter 21

A star is born

When the school day ends—finally!—we stop by Ms. Lonneman's room to bail out our incarcerated friend, Humphrey.

She has his jail cell on her desk, and is feeding him baby carrots when we walk into the lab.

"I was hoping you'd forgotten him," she says. "I'm getting kind of attached."

Leigh Ann is standing directly behind me, looking over my shoulder. "He *is* kind of cute," she admits. "Do you think I could . . . hold him?"

Ms. Lonneman takes Humphrey from the cage and places him in Leigh Ann's (trembling) hands.

Leigh Ann cradles him gently, her impossibly perfect face breaking into a huge grin. "I can feel his whiskers when he sniffs me. And his tiny little claws, holding on."

I nudge Becca with my elbow. "I think you're right. This is a sure sign of the apocalypse."

Field Marshal Margaret musters the troops. "Okay, time to go, everyone. We have a . . . job to do."

"Oh?" inquires Ms. Lonneman.

"Not a job, really," says Margaret. "More like an assignment."

"Thanks for taking care of Humphrey," I say.

"Anytime," Ms. Lonneman says with a wink. "And we won't let Sister Bernadette know what we're up to."

Now that Leigh Ann has Humphrey, she won't let him go. She stashes him in a zippered pocket for the frigid walk to Eighty-First Street. Because we couldn't risk taking a full bottle of wine to school—a live rat is one thing, but the wine? Way too hard to explain to Sister Bernadette!—Margaret and I dropped it off with Shelley early in the morning.

The setting sun is well hidden by thick gray clouds when we knock on the door at the house on Eighty-Second Street. Shelley gives the wine bottle to Margaret, who hands it off to Becca, to be hidden away in her backpack.

"Boy, I hope no one else saw that," says Shelley, smiling. "I'll end up in jail. Giving booze to a bunch of kids."

"They'll wonder what kind of a school you're going to open, that's for sure," says Becca.

"Well, this is it. Wish us luck," I say.

"Good luck, girls. And thank you for trying, even if you fail."

"Oh, we won't fail," I say. "That word is not in the Red Blazer Girls' vocabulary."

"I wish you wouldn't say stuff like that," Becca scolds after Shelley closes the door. "You're just tempting fate to stick it to you. Not to mention that you seem awful sure of yourself for somebody who ought to be sitting in detention right now."

"Thanks for not mentioning that," I say.

"Focus, you two," Margaret orders. "Is everybody ready? Leigh Ann, are you sure you want to hold the rat?"

"His name is Humphrey, and yes, I'm sure." She pats her coat pocket and smiles, satisfied that Humphrey is where he's supposed to be.

"All right, then. Forward, march."

After making sure that there are no other customers inside, we file into GW Antiques and Curiosities, where we are met by Lindsay.

She acts as if she's happy to see us, but I see right through her fake smile: she's annoyed. "Girls! It's been so long. You know, I figured with Christmas and everything going on, you just . . . gave up on . . . well, you know."

"Oh no," says Margaret, wandering around the shop and pretending to be interested in a heavy glass paperweight. "We've been quite busy, actually. We got to know Shelley—the woman who worked for Mr. Dedmann, remember? Did you realize that she graduated from our school? Small world, isn't it?"

"Oh. Yes, I suppose it is."

"Yeah, and she let us do a lot of looking around over there at the house," I say. "You won't believe the things we found—"

"Or what we learned about Mr. Dedmann," Margaret says. She pauses before sticking the knife in. "Did you know that he was a spy?"

Lindsay does her best to hide her surprise/shock/horror/anger/disbelief, but she's no Meryl Streep; I swear you can see steam coming out of her ears.

And then Becca sticks in the second knife.

From her backpack, she takes out the bottle of wine. "Check this out," she says. "From 1949! There's a whole bunch of these. You know, I thought they'd be spoiled by now, but then Sophie's dad told us that wine is actually better when it's old. Who knew?"

"We were kind of hoping you could tell us how much it's worth," Margaret says.

Lindsay is dumbfounded, and can't take her eyes off the bottle. "B-but that's impossible. He said you needed . . . C-can I show that to . . . someone?" she asks.

"Mr. Klinger? Sure, as long as he's willing to come here. I'm not letting this baby out of my hands," says Becca.

Lindsay takes out her cell phone and retreats into

the back room, where we hear snippets of her sniping at him.

"How should I know if it's real? Just get over here. Now!" she hisses.

Through the front windows, I watch as Marcus Klinger exits his shop, locks the front door, and scurries, ratlike, across the street—carrying, as we had hoped, Mr. Dedmann's walking stick. He barges through the door to Winterbottom's shop, freezing when his eyes land on the bottle in Becca's hands.

"Where did you get that?" he snarls. "Let me see it."

Becca holds it out as if she's going to hand it to him, but then reconsiders and quickly pulls it back, hiding it under her coat.

"How do we know we can trust you?" Margaret asks. "Before we let you see the bottle, we need some collateral. Something like . . . that." She points at the walking stick, gripped so tightly by Klinger that the knuckles of his right hand are white.

"Ha! Just as I thought," he says. "It's a trick. Well, I'm onto you girls. What did you do, buy an empty bottle at a wine shop?"

Margaret ignores him and removes an envelope from her bag. "Oh, I almost forgot. Something else we found." She holds it so that Klinger can see the handwriting on the outside. Rebecca, master forger, has copied the handwriting perfectly. It reads:

Last Will and Testament of C. Dedmann
Garrison Applewood, Esq.

Klinger suddenly looks as if somebody has drained all the blood from his body. He tries to speak, but his lips and tongue seem incapable of movement.

I take advantage of his temporary paralysis. "You know, I'm a book person, just like you, Mr. Klinger. There's nothing like a great read. And, well, let me tell you, this was some interesting reading. Did you know that Mr. Dedmann wrote a new will? Of course, you must have; you two were so close. Strange, though, that he decided to leave everything to Shelley."

"Well, not so strange," says Margaret. "She *is* his great-granddaughter, you know."

I swear that if I had so much as exhaled in their general direction, it would have knocked Klinger and Lindsay to the ground.

Enter Gordon Winterbottom, stage right.

"What, in the name of St. Francis, is going on here?" he growls, storming out of his office. At the sight of four red-blazered girls, he stops and points a crooked finger directly at me. "Y-you! What are you doing here? You and your . . . friends are not welcome here. After what you did to me, you're lucky I'm not calling the police."

He looks so furious that I seriously start to doubt Margaret's plan. There is no way he is going to help us.

"It's okay, Gordon," says Klinger, recovering from the initial shock and trying to play it cool. "They aren't after you. They're attempting to pull a fast one on me this time. But it's not going to work."

Gordon moves right next to Klinger, just as Margaret had instructed, giving me hope that he hasn't abandoned us for a twisted revenge plot of his own.

"Whatever you do," he says to Klinger, "do not trust them. Don't let them out of your sight for a second. I learned that the hard way. They're devious, evil little girls. Bad seeds, every one."

Okay, Mr. W., we get the point. You're laying it on a little thick. Seriously? Evil?

"What's this all about?" Gordon asks.

"This," says Becca, juggling the wine bottle from hand to hand in higher and higher arcs.

"Stop that this instant, you idiot!" Klinger cries. "If that really is a 1949 Château Latour, it's worth thousands of dollars."

"What, this bottle?" Becca asks, swinging it over her head and then letting it fly—directly at Marcus Klinger!

It was supposed to be a nice, gentle toss, but Becca has improvised a little, launching the first French wine-satellite into orbit. As it floats high above his head, Marcus Klinger reaches up for it, moving faster than he's probably moved in years. Lindsay wails. Gordon gasps. And Klinger . . . catches it, fumbles with it for a second, and then finally latches on to it, mere inches before it hits the hardwood floor.

Meanwhile, Gordon reaches down and picks up the walking stick that Klinger has dropped in his frenzy to save the wine (and his own head), and Leigh Ann, pretending to tie her shoe, suddenly screams, "RAT!" loud enough to rattle the windowpanes. Humphrey scuttles across Lindsay's feet, instantly transforming her into a sobbing, foot-stomping banshee.

"What?" Gordon cries. "Where is it?"

"I think it went thataway!" screams Leigh Ann. It's not hard to believe she's terrified; a few hours ago, she *was* terrified of rats. Now, though, it's just darn good acting.

As good as she is, however, there is one performer in this little drama who is even more deserving of the Best Performance Award. Ladies and gentlemen, I present to you Mr. Gordon Winterbottom: he runs in the direction Leigh Ann pointed, swinging the stick back and forth like a maniac. Then we watch in wonder as he drops to the floor, reaching under an old desk and swearing like a sailor.

"I'll get you, you little—"

With Humphrey safely tucked away in my coat pocket, Gordon, still on his hands and knees, continues the hunt for his nemesis behind an overstuffed chair in the back corner of the shop. More banging and swearing, followed by a few seconds of silence, and then . . . . "Blast! He got away. There's a hole in the wall by the radiator."

"Y-you mean, he's still . . . out there?" Lindsay asks, shivering.

"Not for long," says Gordon, climbing to his feet. "I'll get some traps and poison. I'll smoke him out if I have to." He hands the walking stick back to Klinger, who has been cradling the bottle of wine while all that was going on.

"Oh, right. Thanks." He looks it over carefully, checking the silver handle to make sure it's really his stick.

"Beautiful walking stick, by the way," says Gordon. "Hope I didn't damage it. Looks like an antique."

Klinger eyes him suspiciously and grasps the handle firmly. "Yes. Yes, it is quite old. Unlike this bottle of wine," he adds. "Nice try, girls. It's quite obvious that this bottle has been tampered with; for one thing, there's no capsule over the cork. A bottle like this one would have a wrapping of lead foil over the top of the cork. What's inside, grape juice?"

"Kool-Aid, actually," Margaret admits.

"I told you, Klinger," says Gordon. "They're calculating and conniving little miscreants. How they've managed to pull the wool over Sister Bernadette's eyes, I will never know."

"I think you give them too much credit," says Klinger. "They're not nearly as clever as they think they are."

As he says those words, however, he can't take his eyes off the envelope in Margaret's hand.

"I don't suppose you'd let me take a look at that," he says.

"You suppose right," Margaret says. "This is going straight to Mr. Applewood. Carbon paper. Funny stuff, huh?"

Klinger's eyes narrow, his head tilts to one side, and I read his mind: How does she know about the carbon paper?

He starts to hand the bottle of faux wine to me, but I push it right back to him. "You keep it, Mr. Klinger. To remember us not-so-clever girls."

He gives us a little smirkle (you know the look: half smile, half smirk) and walks out the door without a word, swinging his walking stick as if he hasn't a care in the world.

Lindsay, still shaken up, pulls on her coat and announces to Gordon that she is going home. I suspect, however, that there will be a rather lengthy stop at a pub on the way there.

As soon as Lindsay is out of sight, Margaret goes to the overstuffed chair in the corner and reaches underneath.

"How did I do?" Mr. Winterbottom asks.

Margaret's smile brightens up the whole room. "Perfect."

Chapter 22

Busted!

We promise Gordon that we'll be in touch, and leave GW Antiques and Curiosities a moment later. Just in case Marcus Klinger is watching from across the street, we tumble out the front door, acting (okay, maybe over-acting) as if we've been kicked out.

"Your store stinks, anyway," I say, shaking my fist at the door.

"Yeah! And good luck with your rat problem," adds Leigh Ann.

As we walk past Dedmann's house, Shelley opens the front door and steps into the cold winter air without a coat.

"Well?"

Margaret gives her a thumbs-up. "We're good to go. We have some work to do tonight, and then we'll be back here tomorrow at three-thirty."

Shelley clasps her hands together and closes her eyes. "I can't believe it. It's actually going to happen."

"Let's not count our chickens yet," says Margaret. "There's still a lot that can go wrong, and if we don't find the real will, it's not going to matter. To be honest, we need a little luck for all this to work."

I know. Totally not fair leaving you hanging like that, right? Well, at least I know you're paying attention. At the end of the last chapter, Margaret had just announced that whatever was under that chair in Mr. Winterbottom's shop was perfect. And now it's time to reveal the secret, the way we completely, thoroughly, and utterly outsmarted Mr. Sturm & Drang himself, Marcus Klinger. (If you already figured out how we did it, well done, my friend!)

When we get to my apartment, Margaret sets a small yogurt container filled with our homemade Play-Doh on the kitchen table. We surround it, admiring Mr. Winterbottom's work.

"You know, I wasn't a hundred percent sure we could trust him," I say, "but he was crazy good in there. And this . . . it's amazing that he did this while he was back there screaming at that imaginary rat."

Mr. Winterbottom's job, you see, was to make an impression of the walking stick's tip in the Play-Doh—without anyone realizing it. Margaret had left the yogurt container on the table next to the glass paperweight in which she had feigned interest. Once Gordon had the stick (thanks to the airborne wine bottle), all he had to do was find the yogurt cup, remove the protective rubber end from the walking stick, carefully press the brass tip deep into the Play-Doh, and then remove it without twisting or turning—all of which he performed flawlessly.

"That is one crazy old dude," says Becca.

"I know, right?" I say. "I was just glad that he wasn't really chasing Humphrey. He would have scared the little guy to death."

"Well, I'll say one thing about him," says Leigh Ann, grinning coyly. "He certainly knows how to make a first . . . impression."

"Nice," says Margaret. "Well done, Leigh Ann."

Becca disagrees. "That's baaaad."

"Ignore her," I tell Leigh Ann. "It's funny. She's just mad because she didn't think of it."

Margaret takes the two tubes of epoxy from her bag and sets them on a section of newspaper that she has spread out on the table. "Okay, back to work. I mixed up a little sample batch last night to make sure." She holds up a tiny epoxy "pop" molded in a plastic bottle cap, with a toothpick for a stick. "I smeared the inside of the cap with oil so I could remove the epoxy after it hardened. Check it out—it's like rock."

We take turns squeezing and tapping on the bottle cap, convincing ourselves that Margaret's plan is going to work.

Using a plastic spoon, Margaret measures out ten spoonfuls of the first component of the epoxy into an empty yogurt cup, and then two of the second component. Then she stirs the two together for several minutes, checking the texture by lifting spoonfuls of the stuff and letting it drip back into the cup.

"It's ready," she says. "I'm really nervous. It has to get into all the little nooks and crannies or this isn't going to work."

"It will work," I insist. "It's an amazing plan."

Slowly, carefully, she pours the epoxy into the inch-deep hole in the Play-Doh, using a toothpick to help guide it into every crevice, every little notch of the impression. When it is full, she taps the cup on the table a few times, and then pours a little more in and levels it off. As a final step, she presses the head of an inch-long wood screw down into the wet epoxy, leaving the pointy, threaded part sticking straight up.

"What's that for?" Becca asks.

"That's how we're going to attach it to this," she says, lifting up a piece of wooden broomstick. "After the epoxy hardens, we pop it out, screw the tip into the end of the broomstick, and—ta-da!—we have our key. But, for now, we wait. We have to give it a couple of hours, to be safe."

"Where did you get the idea for this?" Leigh Ann asks.

"One of those *CSI* shows," Margaret admits. "They're always making plaster casts of footprints and tire prints. I figured we could do the same thing, but make it tougher, so we can use it as a key. Simple, really."

Yeah, if you're a brainiac.

Rebecca and Leigh Ann can't wait around for the unveiling, so two hours later, my mom and I are the only spectators as Margaret grasps the end of the buried wood screw and gives it a good tug.

The epoxy pops right out, leaving the Play-Doh as good as new. Margaret holds up a nearly perfect replica of the walking stick's brass tip.

"Holy smokes," I say. "It worked. You could even make another one."

"Tell me again what this is for," Mom says. "It's some kind of key?"

"Yep. It's for—"

But Mom has lost interest, at least temporarily, as she interrupts my story: "Sophie, what is in your pocket?"

Uh-oh.

The tale of how Humphrey happens to be living in my pocket has an unexpected ending. Mom listens silently to the whole thing, and then, without warning, stands up and tosses my coat at me. "Put that on right now, young lady."

"Wh-what? Why? Where are we going?"

"We are going to this Coffeeteria place, where you

are going to return that young man's rat and apologize to him."

"Mom! You're not serious. I was going to take him back tomorrow. I swear."

"Not good enough," she says. "I know you, and you were going to just slip him right back into the pocket he came from, weren't you?"

"Well, um . . . yeah. What's wrong with that?"

"Sophie! Everything's wrong with that. If you're going to run all over town doing these good deeds like some superhero-in-a-red-blazer, your behavior has to be beyond reproach! And don't tell me that the end justifies the means. Perkatory closing is not the end of the world. Humphrey's owner probably thinks he's dead, for goodness' sake. He goes back tonight."

"I'll see you in the morning," says Margaret, pulling on her own coat. "Good luck."

"Thanks," I say glumly.

Mom walks briskly all the way to Coffeeteria as I struggle to keep up with her.

"I can't believe we're doing this," I grumble under my breath as we go inside.

Mom grumbles right back, "Well, I can't believe my daughter is a thief. Now, where is he?"

"Right here," I say, patting my pocket.

"Not the rat. Him. The manager him."

"Oh. Over there, behind the counter. Jeff."

Mom puts her hands on my shoulders and propels

me across the room. At least the place isn't busy: a few of the tables are occupied by the laptop brigade, but most are empty as I pass them on the way to the counter.

"Can I help you?" asks Jeff.

I avoid eye contact, focusing instead on the selection of nuts and chocolate right in front of me. "Um, hi. Yeah. I, uh, need to talk to you."

"Is there something wrong?" He glances over my head at the half-filled tables. "Is somebody bothering you?"

"No, no. Nothing like that. I just, um, have something that, um, belongs to you." I point with my eyes at my right blazer pocket, where I am lifting Humphrey high enough to reveal his face and those adorable whiskers.

Jeff's eyes almost pop out of his head. "Kirby! Is that you?"

At the sound of his voice, Humphrey/Kirby clambers up my arm and I manage to hand him off to Jeff, who tucks him safely away before everyone in the place gets an eyeful of rat.

"Where did you find him?" he asks.

I take a deep breath, and then another.

"Yeah. About that. I kind of . . . took him. From your pocket."

"You took my pet rat? Why?"

"It's a crazy story. See, I was mad because you guys opened right across from Perkatory, which is my favorite place, and then they closed because the inspector saw a rat, but I was convinced that you were involved because my boyfriend, well, he's really not my boyfriend, he's actually just a really, really good friend who is a boy, and well, anyway, he was in here one day and saw that you had a pet rat that you kept in your pocket, so I figured you planted him in Perkatory so the inspector would be sure to find him"—another breath—"and so I kidnapped him but then I forgot to send the ransom note because I have a lot of stuff going on right now, and then I found out that Perkatory is going to open tomorrow, anyway, so I knew I had to return him to you, and I took really good care of him except for that one time I kind of lost him, but we found him, and everything is fine, and he's back and safe and I'm really, really sorry." Huge breath.

He stares at me for a while, shaking his head. "I think I remember you. You were in here right after we opened. You kept talking about how great Perkatory was. Sorry, is."

"Yeah, that was me," I admit.

He looks toward the door. "Is that your mom back there?" he asks.

"Yeah," I admit.

"She making you do this?"

I nod. "But I was going to bring him back to you tomorrow, I swear. I would have just snuck him back into your pocket."

"I guess the important thing is that Kirby's okay," he says. "Serves me right for bringing him to work. I rescued him from a lab at school. They were going to use him for . . . Well, you don't want to know. You really thought I planted him to shut down Perkatory?"

I nod sheepishly. "Sort of."

"It's not a bad idea. Maybe if I had thought of it, they wouldn't be reopening so soon."

"So we're, you know, cool?"

He shrugs. "Just tell me one thing. What is so great about Perkatory? I've been in there, and, I'm sorry, but the coffee is terrible. The hot chocolate comes from an envelope. The pastries are usually stale. And on top of that, the place is a dump."

"Yeah, but it's *my* dump, you know what I mean?"

He smiles. "I think I do, kid. Well, look, when you get tired of their crappy food and lousy coffee, give us another try." He turns around, and I start to walk away, thinking we're done.

"Wait a second," he says, squirting four-inch-high caps of whipped cream onto two cups of hot chocolate. "These are on the house. Tell your mom I said thanks. What's your name, anyway, kid?"

"Sophie. Sophie St. Pierre."

"Well, Sophie St. Pierre, I'll bet life is never dull when you're around."

"Thanks," I say, smiling because that's the second time I've heard that in two days. "I try."

Chapter 23

All right, so maybe it was closer to half a gazillion

As I lay awake in bed, hopped up on the caffeine from Coffeeteria's amazing hot chocolate, I realize (a little reluctantly) that Mom had been right. Again. In my head, I had been justifying my actions, but deep down, I'm pretty sure I knew they were wrong. I hope so, anyway.

The next thing I know, I'm sitting outside a café in Paris, a bottle of Orangina and my just-barely-held-together-by-tape copy of *A Tree Grows in Brooklyn* on the table before me. Behind me, I hear a scooter's engine revving and turn my head, fully expecting to see Raf's million-dollar smile. The sun is in my eyes, and as I hold up a hand to block the glare, the driver of the scooter removes his helmet. Slowly, he turns enough for me to see his face, and I almost fall off my chair.

"Mr. Winterbottom?"

But he's not looking at me; his eyes land on a woman sitting a few tables away. As I slip my dark sunglasses on so I can stare at her without being too obvious, she turns toward the waiter, tossing her head and laughing at something he says.

"Winnie?"

If she hears me, she doesn't show it, refocusing her attention on the glossy gossip magazine resting on her lap. Still straddling his scooter, Gordon revs the engine again, watches her for a few seconds longer, and then disappears into the Paris traffic.

When I turn back around, the seat across the table from me is occupied: naturally, it's the face of the woman I've come to know as St. Veronica, and she's wearing a strange expression.

"It's up to you, Sophie. The answer is in the stars."

Friday, the last day of school before Christmas vacation, has finally arrived, and not a moment too soon. I love St. V's, but even I need a break every now and then. In two days, I'll be getting on a plane with Mom and Dad and heading to France to see Dad's side of the family—and I can't wait.

"You won't believe the dream I had last night," I tell Margaret on the way to school. "I don't know if it was that crazy hot chocolate, or feeling guilty about that whole thing with Humphrey, or what, but Gordon and Winnie were in my dream, in Paris."

"Wow. That's scary. What were they doing?" she asks, cringing at what she's afraid I might say.

I tell her about the scooter, and Winnie, and St. Veronica's observation about the stars, and then ask, "What do you think it means? *What* is up to me? The answer to *what* is in the stars?"

"Somehow, the Winterbottoms' fate and yours have gotten . . . intertwined. Maybe it's because it's the winter solstice, but there is definitely some weird, cosmic stuff going on. Very Scrooge and Marley; it's like the universe is leveling everything out. First Livvy Klack saves your neck, and then Gordon Winterbottom totally pulls off the performance of the year to help us out. Bizarre. But it's like I said—anybody can see that Gordon and Winnie belong together. Apparently, somebody out there has decided that it's your job to make it happen."

"Okay, then . . . how? Help me."

"Start with Elizabeth. Call her. I'll bet she'll have some ideas. After all, she must know Winnie as well as anyone. Remember how she interrogated us the first time we met? I guarantee she did that to Winnie, too."

"Hey, that's a good idea," I say.

Margaret holds the school door open for me. "It's funny. After all these years, you still sound surprised when you say that."

At the morning assembly, our production of Mr. Eliot's play, *The Merry Gentlemen,* is sandwiched between the two halves of the choir concert: the somber first part and the everybody-sing-along-at-the-top-of-your-lungs finale.

And somehow, despite all Mr. Eliot's last-minute changes and incessant worrying, we pull it off. After the final bow, the students in his honors English class drag Mr. Eliot onto the stage and hand him a wrapped package, which we insist that he open in front of everyone. He tears off the paper and holds up a leather-bound edition of Charles Dickens's *David Copperfield,* one of his favorite books.

"It's beautiful," he says as he leafs through the pages, his eyes turning moist.

"You like it?" Margaret asks.

"Love it," he says. "You really shouldn't have. . . . Thank you—all of you. I'm going to reread it over the break."

Margaret pulls Livvy front and center by the arm. "Livvy found it," she says. "We looked all over, but couldn't find anything good. Livvy saw this online, but it was only available in England. Lucky for you, her parents just happen to be in London, and she had them send it here."

"Well, it's perfect. You chose wisely, Livvy."

As we scamper off the stage, Livvy beams, glowing with the satisfaction of her good deed. "Are you and your friends going to be at your usual table at lunch today?"

"Yeah, I guess," I say. "Why?"

"Oh, nothing. I just want to make sure I see you before you leave for vacation," she says, and then runs off to sit with some of her old friends.

• • •

An hour later, over red-and-green cupcakes and cartons of milk, we hold the first annual RBGGE (Red Blazer Girls Gift Exchange). Back in November, after much debate, we made a historic decision: we would draw names and buy only one gift, "secret Santa" style. The idea, of course, was that instead of spending a gazillion dollars, we would spend only a third of a gazillion.

So, how did that work out? you ask.

Well, smarty-pants, just see for yourself.

When we've cleared away our mess, we set the four wrapped packages on the table.

"How do we decide who goes first?" I ask.

Margaret slides her package across the table to me. "How about you? Go ahead, get it started, Soph."

I'm not about to wait for someone to protest. I yank the paper off the red cardboard box and look inside, where I find a beautiful leather journal (the same one Margaret had seen me admiring), a bottle of ink (red, of course), and my very own fountain pen!

"Oh my gosh, it's perfect!" I say, throwing my arms around her. "I love it!"

"The pen isn't an antique," she says, "but it writes beautifully. The guy at the store let us try a bunch of them. This was our favorite."

"Okay, enough about Sophie. Leigh Ann is next," says Becca.

"Yay!" cries Leigh Ann. "Gimme, gimme!"

She tears the wrapping from the custom-made, one-of-a-kind scrapbook that Becca has been working on for weeks. The cover, cut from a thin sheet of plywood, is painted with images of the four of us: Margaret playing the violin, Becca behind an easel, me with my guitar, and, in the center, Leigh Ann in an elegant ballet pose.

"You made this? Becca, it's amazing!"

"Look inside," I say.

Leigh Ann turns back the cover. Inside are four pages, front and back, covered with pictures and mementos from her first four months at St. Veronica's, followed by a couple of dozen more blank pages waiting for her to fill them in.

"Remember what Frodo told Sam at the end of *The Lord of the Rings*?" Becca says. "The last pages are for you."

Leigh Ann's eyes well up with tears and she practically tackles Becca. "Thank you so much. I'm going to fill it up and keep it forever. Here, Margaret, open this. I can't be the only one crying."

"Uh-oh," says Margaret, shaking the small box. "I don't want to open it if it's going to make me cry."

"Tough," says Becca. "Open it."

Margaret removes the paper without tearing it, folds it, and sets it aside. She takes a deep breath and lifts the lid from a small wooden box, revealing a pair of simple, yet elegant men's cuff links, made of gold and onyx. Her brow wrinkles as she ponders them silently for a few seconds.

"Look underneath," says Leigh Ann.

Margaret pulls up the velvet divider and removes a wrinkled black-and-white photograph. It is a picture of her grandparents on their wedding day.

"Now look really close," I say.

Margaret bites the first knuckle of her right hand to prevent herself from crying, but it's a battle she's going to lose. Once she realizes the significance of the cuff links, she can't take her eyes off them.

"Are they really . . . ? But how?"

"When your grandmother was here, we asked her if there was anything of your grandfather's that you could have," Leigh Ann explains. "She told us about these, but said that one was broken. We got her to send them, and then I got the broken one fixed. So, I guess they're kind of from your *babcia* and me."

"Well, thank you . . . both. I love them. Now that I see them, I remember him wearing them . . . to my birthday party. It was the first time I ever saw anyone wear a shirt with cuff links."

I hold up Becca's gift. "Last again, Becca."

"Just hand it over, St. Pierre." She grabs it from me and rips the wrapping off in one swipe. She stares at it for a second, speechless.

"No way," she says, finally.

"Let me see," says Leigh Ann. "I've heard about it, but I never got to see it."

Becca holds up an antique silver picture frame containing a beautiful photograph of her father. He's standing amid the machinery of his print shop—so young and handsome that it's impossible to believe that he's been gone for five years.

"I've never even seen this picture before," she says. "Where did you get it?"

"Well, your mom helped us out a little," I admit. "It was kind of dumb luck. I asked her about pictures, and she found a few, but then she found a roll of film from your dad's camera that had never been developed. She'd completely forgotten that he had asked her to take some pictures of him: they were going to be for an ad in one of the Chinatown papers. She couldn't believe it when she got them developed. We liked this one best, so we took the negatives to a photo lab, and they made us this print. And the frame came from Mr. Winterbottom's shop. I saw it the first time we were in there. It's silver, so Lindsay said you're going to have to keep it polished. Do you like it?"

"It's . . ."

And then . . . well, I think you can guess what happens next. And that way, Becca can't get mad at me for divulging her deepest, darkest secret.

• • •

The wrapping paper and ribbons have been thrown out and the tears wiped away when Livvy joins us at our table and opens her laptop.

"Is . . . everything all right?" she asks as she takes in our red eyes and runny noses. "Did something bad happen?"

"No, we're fine," I say. "We just exchanged gifts and it got a little—"

"Oh, right," she says. "Well, that's good timing. I have something for you guys."

Panicky looks zigzag around the table, and Livvy holds up a hand. "Don't worry," she says, laughing. "I didn't expect you to get me anything. And this is just a little . . . thank-you, for helping me get my . . . act together." She spins the laptop so the screen is facing us.

Bright red letters pop up on the screen:

LIVE! FROM PERKATORY
IN NEW YORK CITY . . .
THE BLAZERS!

What follows is a remarkably professional-looking music video of us, pieced together from some of our Friday-night performances. We're playing the "hit song" that I wrote—"The Apostrophe Song"—inspired by Mr. Eliot's lesson and group project on apostrophes. (That was also, ironically, the project in which Livvy burned us to the ground when she "accidentally" told us the wrong day for our class presentation. When Mr. Eliot called on us, she was the only one prepared. What followed was not pretty.)

"How did you do this?" I ask as I watch myself play the song's final chord. "I never saw you at Perkatory, and definitely not with a camera."

Livvy smiles. "It wasn't me. I got your friend Malcolm Chance to do it. He filmed it two weeks in a row, and then I put it all together. Do you like it?"

"It's great," says Leigh Ann. "We look—and sound—like a real band."

"You *are* a real band," says Livvy. "And I was, um, kind of hoping you would let me try out. I've been playing piano for six years. I'm not great, but I learn new stuff pretty quickly. You don't have to answer now; just think about it, and maybe after vacation I can show you what I can do."

"We *have* been thinking about adding a keyboard," says Becca. "You know, to give us more sound. We'd have to get an electric piano, though—there's no room for a real one at Perkatory."

"So . . . you guys will think about it? Seriously?"

"Yeah, absolutely," I say.

"That is awesome!" Livvy says, beaming. "I'm gonna practice all your songs over the break. I can't wait!"

Chapter 24

In which my dad gets a glimpse of his version of heaven

The bell rings—Christmas vacation has officially begun! We all have something else on our minds, though, as we pack up our bags and exit the building for a two-week break: today we learn the truth about Mr. Dedmann's secret cellar. The codes have been broken, and the walking stick has been duplicated. All that remains is for us to enter the combination—and hope.

We've invited Livvy and Raf to join us for the great unveiling, and after a quick hot dog at the Papaya King on Eighty-Sixth, we walk back down to Dedmann's house on Eighty-Second. Shelley lets us in, and as I kneel down to pet Bertie, she introduces us to a middle-aged man in a camel hair overcoat.

"This is Mr. Garrison Applewood, Mr. Dedmann's lawyer," she says. "And these are the girls—and some friends—I was telling you about. They've been a huge help."

Margaret holds up her right hand, her fingers crossed. "Let's just hope that we've been right about everything."

"Nice to meet you girls . . . and boy," Mr. Applewood says. "I understand that you have been working on this day and night. I'm sure you realize by now that Mr. Dedmann was a bit of a character. I knew him for thirty years, but I can't say I know anything about him. He had all this, but I can't tell you how he got it. Never had a job that I knew of. Lived incredibly simply—he didn't travel, didn't eat out. When Shelley told me what you'd discovered—that he was actually someone named Kaspar Neuner, who was a notorious World War II spy—I was shocked. I had no idea."

"Well, I suppose everybody has some secrets," Shelley says. "His were just . . . bigger than most."

The doorbell rings; Bertie barks once, and everybody jumps. We're all a little on edge.

Shelley looks out the peephole in the door. "It's a man. . . . I don't recognize him."

"Let me see," I say. "It's probably my dad." A quick peek confirms it, and I open the door. "Hey, Dad!"

Dad comes in, and when Bertie finally leaves him alone, I introduce him to Shelley and Mr. Applewood. "I thought it might be nice to have someone here who knows something about wine," I say. "Dad's kind of an expert—he's a chef, and he's from France. He's the one who told us about that bottle that Shelley found."

Dad shakes his head at the memory. "Château La-tour, 1949. *Fantastique.*"

I suppose I should mention that poor Dad knows next to nothing about why I asked him to come. I told him about Curtis Dedmann and Shelley, but I may have left out a few teensy details—like the fact that Dedmann was a German spy, and somehow had enough money to build a huge house with an even bigger wine cellar, which might just be full of expensive wine. That's all.

"Sophie didn't tell us that she invited you," says Margaret.

"She is full of secrets, this one," says Dad, patting me on the head.

"Shall we go downstairs?" Shelley asks. "For the big moment?"

Down the spiral stairs we go, Margaret leading the way. When she gets to the cellar, she walks to the other end, running her hand across the top of the round table.

"Beethoven's Nine," she says, smiling. "Kaspar Neuner. Nine chairs. Sophie and I did a little research on German names last night, and guess what we found out? 'Neun' is German for 'nine,' so 'Neuner' means, literally, 'a niner.' As in one who is part of a council made up of nine members. All the nines—the tiles, the address, everything—it was his clever little joke on the world. It's just like the words written in the stars. The secret to his identity was right under everyone's noses all along."

She opens her backpack, takes out a one-foot length

of broomstick, and unwraps the paper that has been protecting the epoxy tip that is a perfect copy of the bottom of Mr. Dedmann's walking stick.

"Boy, I hope this works," she says as we gather around her.

"Julius Caesar is first," I say. "And you turn him clockwise."

Margaret kneels down on the floor directly over Caesar's medallion. She blows the dust out of the indentation in the center, lines up the grooves and notches of the key, and gently pushes it into place. "So far, so good," she says. "It fits perfectly." We hold our breath as she slowly, slowly, slowly turns the key, and listen as the machinery of the lock beneath us and in the walls clicks several times, followed by a whirring sound and one final *ker-chunk*.

All nine of us breathe in simultaneously.

"That's one," I say. "Now for our Muse. Well, Leigh Ann's Muse, anyway. Terpsichore, counterclockwise."

Margaret takes the key to the next set of black tiles and settles in over Terpsichore's medallion.

Click, click, click, CLICK.

Whirrrrrr. Errk. Whirrrrrrrrr.

Ker-chunk. Ker-CHUNK.

Breathe.

"All right, Venus, you're up!" says Becca, racing Margaret to the final block of tiles and rubbing the medallion in the center. "Don't let us down."

The key goes in.

Silence.

More silence.

Then, faintly, the sound of a clock ticking all around us, growing louder and louder: *tickticktickticktickticktick-ticktick-ticktickTICKTICKTICKTICK . . . errrrrrr-kkkkKER-CHUNK!*

The wall at the back end of the house shudders for a second, but then the center section starts to move before our eyes, pivoting like a revolving door and leaving two openings, each about three feet wide. As the doors come to a stop, lights turn on automatically, and we all stand in the center of the room, frozen to the marble tiles.

"Holy crap," I say.

"That was amazing," says Leigh Ann.

Becca is the first to make a move for the opening. "Let's check it out!"

"Don't touch anything," Margaret warns.

"Yeah, Bec," I say. "You break it, you buy it."

"Look at this place," says Dad, stepping inside. "It is immaculate. Temperature- and humidity-controlled. It must go back twenty-five or thirty feet in that direction, and there's a passageway all the way around the base-ment. There must be four or five thousand bottles. Who *was* this guy?"

I glance at Margaret, who, from the look on her face, is making mental calculations. Five thousand bottles times ten dollars, times a hundred dollars . . . Her eyes grow wide as those numbers start to get seriously, well, serious.

An antique wheeled cart, its sides painted with clusters of grapes, sits just inside the opening in the wall. On it are three wooden cases of wine—one each from Bordeaux, Burgundy, and the Loire Valley—and tucked in between two of the cases, nearly out of sight, is a single manila envelope on which Mr. Dedmann has written: "For Garrison Applewood, in appreciation for his years of service."

Shelley hands the envelope to Mr. Applewood, who immediately tears it open and removes a single sheet of stationery with a handwritten message and a small, sealed envelope. The suspense builds to an unbearable level as we watch him read the letter with no sign of emotion.

Finally, I can't take it anymore. "What is it? You have to tell us!"

He smiles, holding up the envelope. "It's true. He wrote a new will. This is it. It's been signed and dated and properly witnessed, so it looks perfectly legal to me. Everything he owns, except for these three cases of wine, which are for me, goes to you, Shelley. He says that you will find a journal down here that explains everything in more detail, but you really are his great-granddaughter. At the end of the war, he believed his wife, Venus, and his son, also Kaspar, to have been killed in the bombing of Dresden. He only recently learned that they had survived somehow and emigrated to Canada, thinking that he was dead."

Shelley, sobbing, hugs Mr. Applewood. "Why didn't he just tell me the truth?"

"Well, we can hope to find an answer to that question," Mr. Applewood says, "but I wouldn't count on it. I have a feeling he took a lot of secrets to the grave. Now, let's have a look around down here, to see what he's been hiding all these years."

We all start to move cautiously around the cellar. Everyone except Dad, that is. He is, pardon the cliché, like a kid in the world's greatest candy shop, dashing from stack to stack and running his hands through his hair in utter disbelief.

"Look at this!" he cries. "Two full cases of 1959 Haut-Brion! And one of the '61. Here's Bouscaut! And here's Château Margaux—three cases of the '66! And the Saint-Émilions—Figeac, and Cheval Blanc, and Pavie!"

"He's just making up a bunch of French words, isn't he?" says Becca.

Dad doesn't even hear her; before my very eyes, he drops to his knees and makes the sign of the cross. "Sophie! Come here! *Regardez!* Château Petrus! There must be fifteen, no, twenty cases! *Impossible!*"

"Uh-huh. I'm guessing that's a good one." But he's already moved on to the next stacks, shaking his head and muttering. Now that I've gotten him into this cellar, I'm afraid that I'll never get him out.

Meanwhile, Margaret has gone to the far wall of the cellar, at the back of the house. "Um, guys, come here!" she says. "But watch where you step." She points at muddy footprints on the otherwise pristine tile floor. "Those are new."

"Wh-what? How can they be new?" I ask. "Nobody has been in here for months."

Raf kneels down to make a close inspection. "Hmm. She's right. This is new. It's still wet."

My arms break out in goose bumps, and the skin at the back of my neck tingles.

Leigh Ann latches on to me. "B-but if they're wet—"

"—it means they didn't come in the way we did," Dad says, finishing her thought.

"And look!" cries Margaret. "You can see, right here on the floor, where something was dragged. There were cases of wine stacked all along here. A lot of them, and they're gone!"

Dad picks up one of the loose bottles from the rack before him, then walks completely around the stack before announcing, "These are all Burgundies: Pommard, Chambertin, Corton, Montrachet . . . Clos-de-Vougeot, Nuits-Saint-Georges . . . but nothing in cases."

Margaret has her flashlight out, poking it into every crack in the wall and floor. "This is strange," she says.

"There are two different sets of footprints here. And they all end right . . . here." She stops in front of the racks that line the back wall, near the corner.

"There must be another door," says Livvy.

Margaret runs her hands along the front of the rack. "I don't see how there could . . . Hello! What have we here?"

"What is it?" Leigh Ann asks as we crowd around Margaret.

Margaret lifts a hand-printed card (Meursault 1999) that conceals an undecorated brass medallion with the same "keyhole" in the center as those commemorating the nine planets, Muses, and worthies.

"What are you going to do?" Shelley asks.

Mr. Applewood takes a step backward.

"Um, yeah, Margaret," says Leigh Ann. "How do you know what's on the other side? I mean, it could be . . . anything."

"We didn't know for sure what we'd find in here, either," Margaret replies. "We were pretty sure, maybe, but not positive."

"If you ask me, this whole operation has 'alien invasion' written all over it," says Becca. "This opens a door that leads to their mother ship, which has been buried down here for centuries. I'll bet this Dedmann guy was one of them."

Livvy doesn't know what to make of Becca, and whispers in my ear, "Is she serious?"

"To be honest, I'm never a hundred percent sure," I say.

"He *was* one of them," Margaret says to Becca. "He was a German spy during World War II, remember?"

Becca folds her arms across her chest. "Perfect cover for an alien."

"Well, I'm going to open it," says Margaret, inserting the key into the center of the medallion. She pauses, takes one last look at the faces surrounding her, and turns the key. This time, there's no whirring or clicking or ker-chunking: the door swings open with barely a sound.

Nine anxious, curious people crane their necks to look down the muddy two-foot-wide tunnel that leads away from the wine cellar.

"Cool," says Becca.

"Creepy," says Leigh Ann.

"Shhh!" Margaret hisses. "Listen!"

Leaning in closer and closer, all I hear is the sound of my own nervous breathing . . . until . . . Yes! There it is—a long way off—a voice!

We all step back involuntarily; let's face it, nobody was expecting that.

"Do you have any idea who that might be?" Dad asks me. "I have the feeling you haven't told me everything."

"Wellll, I have an idea, but—"

"It's this guy, Marcus Klinger," says Margaret. "It

has to be. His shop is right"—she points down the tunnel—"there. It's on Eighty-First, just behind this house. He must have believed that we really found the will, and panicked. He knows he's not going to get the house, so he might as well steal all the wine."

"But if he knew about the tunnel all along, why wait until now to steal the wine?" Shelley asks. "He could have taken it months ago."

Margaret's head—I swear!—turns into a giant light-bulb as the truth hits her. "He didn't know about the tunnel until Lindsay showed him those blueprints! Remember, Soph? We were hiding in the elevator and spying on them, and she told him about the plans."

"And he asked her if he could take a closer look!" I say.

Dad holds up a hand to stop us. "Wait, wait, wait. What plans? Who are you talking about?"

"Um, yeah, Dad," I start. "There's actually a lot I didn't tell you."

"And there's no time now," says Margaret. "They're coming!"

Leigh Ann's eyes are big as platters. "Oh my gosh. What are we going to do? What if it's not Klinger?"

Margaret softly closes the tunnel door. "Everyone hide! We need to see who it is, and then—"

"I'll sneak around and shut the door behind them," says Raf.

Dad gives me a what-did-you-get-me-into? look and

ducks behind a stack of wooden wine cases. "Romanée-Conti," he sighs loudly. "If they start shooting, please, God, let them hit me and not the wine."

"Sh-sh-shooting?" stammers Mr. Applewood. "Miss Gallivan, you didn't say anything about . . . You d-don't really think . . . ?"

"No," I say firmly. "We'll be fine."

I mean, we will, won't we?

Chapter 25

When will these crooks learn to stop underestimating us?

And so we wait, hunkered down behind thousand-dollar bottles of wine. Whoever is out there is getting closer, but I still can't distinguish voices through the thick door.

"Sounds like they have a wagon," Leigh Ann says. "Something's squeaking."

"Those are probably the GSRs," says Becca.

"GSRs?" Shelley asks.

"Giant subterranean rodents," Becca answers. "They're all over Manhattan."

"You can't scare me with rat stories anymore," whispers Leigh Ann. "Now that I got to know Humphrey, I realize that rats are only trying to survive, and take care of their families—just like everybody else in the world. And there's no such thing as a GSR. You stole that from that movie with the princess and the giant and that you-killed-my-father-prepare-to-die guy."

"His name is Inigo Montoya. And those were

250

ROUSs—rodents of unusual size," I say. "Totally different creature. These are much bigger. And more dangerous."

Margaret shushes us. "They're right outside," she whispers. "Stay down."

"What is your plan?" Dad asks her.

Margaret smiles, shrugging. "I don't know. I'm . . . improvising."

Something bumps into the door, and a few seconds later it swings wide open. I can't say that I'm shocked when Marcus Klinger—unshaven, filthy, a bit desperate-looking, and holding the walking stick—steps inside. I expected to see him.

"C'mon," he growls. "We still have a long way to go. All this Burgundy has to be moved, and then the Bordeaux. If you want your share, you're going to have to get a little dirty. Stay there! I'll hand the cases to you, and you stack them on the wagon. It's too hard getting it over this threshold. And be careful. If you break it, it comes out of your share."

The second person grunts something unintelligible from the tunnel. From my vantage point, I can see the back wheels of the wagon, and for the next few minutes, Klinger lifts case after case of wine, setting each on the back of the wagon. A pair of dirt-covered hands then pulls it forward and out of sight. Just as I'm getting really frustrated at not being able to see who it is, the helper in the tunnel backs up to the doorway. I can't see his face, but I would know that baggy, dirt-brown suit and those clunky black wingtip shoes anywhere—it's Gordon Winterbottom! For crying out loud!

Margaret reaches the same conclusion at the same moment, because she turns to me with open mouth, upturned hands, and a look that says, "Once a crook, always a crook."

As they continue loading, I try to imagine how this dastardly duo managed to join forces. Seriously, it's like the Joker and Lex Luthor getting together. Apparently, Gordon's performance was even more convincing than I originally thought—he fooled us completely. That old so-and-so must have run over to Sturm & Drang the second we left to tell Klinger what we had done, just so he could really stick it to us! When Klinger heard that we would soon have our own key to the cellar, he panicked and headed for the tunnel. And now my old pal Winterpatootie thinks he's going to get a piece of this million-dollar pie.

Well, you know what? I don't think so!

"Hold it right there, you two!" I shout, surprising everyone—including me.

Klinger spins around so fast that his face is a blur. "What the . . . Where did you . . . ?" (Thankfully, he doesn't drop the case of 1999 Aloxe-Corton he is holding; I hate to think what my dad would have done to him in the face of such senseless destruction—'99 was a very good year, after all.)

But it's Gordon's face that is the real shocker. When I shout, he turns and . . . and . . . well, it's not Gordon Winterbottom at all. It's Lindsay—wearing one of Gordon's old three-sizes-too-big suits.

"Lindsay?" I say. "I thought you were . . . those clothes . . . Winterbottom."

She just stares at me, so filthy and exhausted that she almost seems glad that they've been caught red-, no, make that dirty-handed. She sheds Gordon's suit, which she has been wearing in place of coveralls, and stands before me in her own tasteful (if a bit young for her) clothes . . . and those clunky wingtips.

Klinger, meanwhile, realizes that he's surrounded by the eight of us (Mr. Applewood chooses to remain safely behind the stacks), so he sets down the case of wine and throws his hands high in the air. "Fine. I give up."

"Tsk, tsk," says Margaret. "Look at those grubby hands, Mr. Klinger. I hope you won't be handling any of those nice books in your shop in this condition."

"You girls really are . . . exasperating," he says.

An enormous grin splits Margaret's face. "You know, even if there hadn't been a single bottle of wine back here, it still would have been worth all this effort just to hear you say that."

We spend the next hour lugging cases of wine back from the basement of Sturm & Drang to Mr. Dedmann's secret cellar. Shelley has decided not to involve the police, as long as all the wine is returned, and appoints my dad supervisor of that effort. Dad is a nervous wreck, and there are some cases that he won't even let us kids touch.

"I'd rather do it myself," he says, as if it's his wine! "It's better than watching you drop a case of Romanée-Conti."

The tunnel, we learn from the exhausted, defeated Lindsay, was built by Dedmann for his own escape from the FBI, when they came knocking.

"But they never did," she adds. "He was smarter than they were, I'm afraid. Soon the war was over, and Dedmann was a man without a country, in a sense. He had a fortune, thanks to his years in the black market . . . and nothing to do, no one to fear. He spent the next sixty years pretending to be someone he wasn't."

"And collecting wine," adds Dad.

"If I had to guess," says Lindsay, "I would say that, like most German spies of that time, he spent some time in England and France, where he probably developed a taste for . . . the finer things. Things he wouldn't have found in Germany in the 1920s and '30s."

As I glance around the wine cellar, I wonder: how many more secrets are hidden away, just waiting to be discovered? Something tells me that the Third Wise Man has a few tricks up his sleeve yet.

Leigh Ann looks down the dark length of the tunnel. "There's still one thing I don't get. Why did he dig a tunnel to the bookstore's basement?"

Margaret nods. "Good question." She turns to Klinger. "And why did you wait until now to do anything?"

Lindsay answers for him. "Because he didn't know about the tunnel until I showed him the plans for this house."

Margaret nudges me with an elbow. "See! Just like I said!"

Lindsay continues, "As for the tunnel, it leads there because, one, it's close by, and two, Dedmann owned that building, too. Before he sold it to Marcus's father in the sixties, he walled up the tunnel. By then, he was certain that he would never need it."

"Right there . . . all those years," mutters Klinger. "My own basement. Two measly inches of concrete. And Dedmann never let on."

"His real name was Neuner," says Becca. "Kaspar Neuner."

Klinger's bottom lip trembles, and Lindsay gasps.

"How do you know that?" she asks. "What did you find? Where are his secret files? Please, you have to show me. I've waited years to see them. That man killed my grandfather. They could help me finally prove it."

"I don't know about any secret files," Becca answers. "His name was written in the stars, just like he said it would be. You know the big table with the Milky Way painted on it? It's right there, plain as can be."

As you can imagine, that takes a little explaining.

After we reveal the name written in the Milky Way, Leigh Ann tells Dad, "Sophie's the one who figured it out."

"It wasn't just me," I say modestly. "We all did it. And it was my aunt Noëlle who really deserves the credit."

Dad's head tilts several degrees to the left. "*Ma soeur?* Noëlle? What did she do?"

"She sent me this Christmas card," I say, holding up the "magic" card with the red cellophane.

"Oh. I think I'm getting a headache from trying to keep up with you, Sophie."

"It's never boring, though, is it?" I say, thoroughly satisfied with myself.

"Well, what do you think, Mr. Applewood?" Shelley asks, sweeping her arm around the room and its contents. "Do you think I have enough here to start a nice little art school?"

"And then some," Mr. Applewood answers.

"How about you, Mr. St. Pierre? You're the wine expert here. What do you think?"

Dad scratches his chin. "I think you could open three schools."

Chapter 26

Seriously, I think I'm going to have to draw the kid a picture

When we are certain that all the wine is back where it belongs, we send Klinger and Lindsay scurrying on their way through the tunnel. Dad, meanwhile, finds some scraps of wood to wedge into the doorframe to ensure that there won't be any more unwelcome visitors to the secret cellar.

"And now I think we celebrate," says Shelley. "Upstairs, everyone. I have champagne for the grown-ups and ginger ale for the rest of you. I still can't believe it; I feel like my feet aren't touching the ground. How can I ever thank you girls?"

"Just get this school up and running," Margaret says.

"And give Mr. Winterbottom a chance," I add, feeling a little guilty that I was so quick to assume he had stabbed us in the back. "You know, now that we've kept the world safe from the evil clutches of Marcus Klinger, and since it wasn't Gordon down there helping him, we still have one more job to do."

"Gordon and Winnie?" Margaret asks.

"Yep," I say. "And this time, I have a plan. We have to head down to Elizabeth and Malcolm's when we leave here. Apparently, Malcolm made his famous eggnog and is cooking a giant 'roast beast.' Elizabeth left me a message saying that she remembered something Winnie told her a long time ago. When I called her back, she wouldn't tell me over the phone. I think she just wants to make sure we really come."

Upstairs in the formal dining room, we toast our success with enthusiastic clinking of crystal champagne flutes. After wishing Shelley well in her new life, and promising to keep in touch, we say our good-byes to her; Mr. Applewood; Livvy, whose parents are waiting for her at home (and who promises to meet us Saturday night at Perkatory); and Dad, who has to hurry downtown to the restaurant.

"Nobody will believe me when I tell them what I've seen here," he says, before adding, "Sophie—call your mother and tell her where you're going. And don't be late. And stay with Margaret."

"Don't worry, I'll take care of her," says Margaret.

Rebecca comes between Raf and me, putting her arms around our shoulders. "Yeah, and I'll sit between these two crazy kids."

"Gee, thanks for offering to be my personal chaper-one, Becca," I say, "but Raf has to leave, too."

"'Fraid so," Raf says. "Family stuff."

"You sound thrilled about that," says Leigh Ann.

"I'm gonna end up babysitting a bunch of my cous-ins," he groans. "They're all brats."

I take Raf by the arm. "I, um, need to talk to you. Let's go outside for a minute."

"You want me to go with her, Mr. S.?" Becca says. "You know, just to make sure there's no monkey busi-ness."

"I take back all the nice things I've ever said about you, Becca," I say, slamming the door in her face.

The temperature has dropped in the two hours that we were inside, and we're both shivering as we stand outside Mr. Dedmann's—make that Mr. Neuner's—front door.

"I just want to make sure we're still on for tomor-row," I say. "You *are* going to make it to Perkatory, aren't you?"

"I'll be there, I promise," he says. "Unless—"

"No! No 'unless'! I'm leaving for France on Sunday—for ten days!"

"Okay, okay. If my mom says anything, I'll just tell her . . . something."

"That's better." I lead him out of the porch light and away from the line of sight of the Rebeccarazzi. "So, I guess I'll see you tomorrow?" I say, tilting my head to the side and breaking out my sure-thing, kiss-me-you-fool smile.

Arggghhh! Raf totally misses the signs! He gives me a quick brotherly hug, and bops down the steps, shouting, "See ya tomorrow! Call me!"

Walking into Elizabeth's townhouse is like walking into a scene from a Norman Rockwell painting. The fireplace, crackling and hissing, gives the room a warm, golden glow, aided by the dozen burning candles on the carved mantel. In one corner stands a ten-foot Christmas tree, simply, yet tastefully decorated, with stacks of color-coordinated packages beneath.

Elizabeth, who is famous for her over-the-top outfits, has outdone herself: she's a vision in red-and-green checked slacks and green turtleneck, topped off with the red blazer she bought to match ours—and a Santa hat.

"Girls!" she cries when Malcolm ushers us into the living room. "I was so afraid I wouldn't get to see you all before Christmas. Come and sit in front of the fire—you must be freezing. Now, you've got to have a glass of Malcolm's homemade eggnog." She leans in and whispers, "Pretend you like it even if you don't; otherwise, he'll pout."

"I heard that!" says Malcolm. "But I'm not concerned. It's simply inconceivable that they won't like it. People rave about it."

Maybe it's the atmosphere—the roaring fire, the Christmas tree, being surrounded by my best friends—but Malcolm's eggnog is right up there with the best things I've ever had to drink.

"It's . . . incredible," Leigh Ann says, agreeing with the yummy noises I'm making.

Malcolm thumbs his nose at Elizabeth and sits on the arm of the couch. "Now, don't you have a little something else for these young ladies?" he asks.

"As a matter of fact, I do," says Elizabeth, springing to her feet and running to the tree. She digs into the piles of presents and returns with a single elegantly wrapped gift.

Margaret starts to protest. "You shouldn't have bought us any—"

"Nonsense," says Elizabeth. "It's just a little something I had my friend Susanna put together. She has a small jewelry store downtown."

"Well, go ahead," Malcolm orders. "Open it."

On the count of three, we tear off the paper and pop open the black jewelry box.

Resting on the velvet surface inside is a half-dollar-size bronze coin that has been cut into four equal wedges, with a black silk cord looped through each.

"It's a copy of a piece my father found in France," says Elizabeth. "He was leading an excavation around Rocamadour and it turned up—it's the only one like it. No one knows for sure who the woman is whose face is

261

on it, but when some of the local diggers started calling it the St. Veronica coin, the name stuck. The original is in the Metropolitan Museum, of course."

I remove mine from the box and slip the silk cord around my neck, unable to take my eyes off it. "It's beautiful."

Becca, Margaret, and Leigh Ann put theirs on, too, and we hold the pieces together to complete the circle.

"The fellowship of the ring," says Becca.

"I'm so glad you like them," Elizabeth says, accepting hugs from all four of us.

"We have a little something for you two," says Margaret. "From all of us. Sophie?"

After a rather lengthy archaeological expedition in my book bag, I produce a small envelope, which I hand to Elizabeth.

Before she opens it, she scolds us. "Girls, you should be saving your money instead of spending it on us." She slides a letter opener under the flap and removes the card.

"Well?" says Malcolm. "What is it?"

"A gift certificate to my dad's restaurant," I say. "For a very special dinner for two. Dad says there's only one rule: you have to give him a day's warning so he can put together the most amazing meal ever."

"This is too much," Elizabeth says, her eyes filling with tears. "I've eaten at your father's restaurant; I know how expensive it is. We can't possibly—"

"Don't worry," I say. "We have that under control.

We're trading Dad some labor for food. We—all of us—have a couple of Sundays of cleaning and polishing ahead."

"Promise us that you guys will use it," Margaret says.

"We promise," says Malcolm. "And thank you."

Following the individual and group hugs, we move to the dining room for "the feast of the beast" as Malcolm calls it, and over plates heaped with roast beef, mashed potatoes, assorted vegetables, gravy, and rolls, we share the story of our latest case.

Malcolm is especially intrigued by Mr. Winterbottom's involvement, laughing out loud when I described him on his hands and knees, chasing the "rat" around the antiques shop.

"I may have to reach out to Gordon after New Year's," he says. "Perhaps we've judged him too harshly in the past."

"So, Elizabeth," I say, "you mentioned remembering something about Winnie. . . ."

"Oh, of course!" she says. "I almost forgot. It all came back to me. When she started with me, almost twenty years ago, she told me about how she and Gordon had met. She was working at that German restaurant up on Second Avenue—"

"The Heidelberg?" Margaret asks. "That's where she's working now!"

"Yes, that's the place. She said she knew that Gordon had a crush on her—"

"Did she really say that?" Becca asks. "A crush? On Winnie. There are two words I never thought I'd hear in the same sentence."

Elizabeth smiles. "That was the word she used—I'm certain of it. He would go there almost every day, sometimes twice a day, and he always sat at one of her tables. She said he gained about twenty pounds! Well, they would talk and talk, and one day she told him about growing up out in the country in Germany, and how beautiful the stars were. Of all the things she missed because she lived in New York, it was the stars she longed for the most.

"The very next day, he finally worked up the courage to ask her out—it was a beautiful Saturday afternoon, she said, and after a nice lunch, they went for a walk in the park, and then . . . I just love this part . . . he told her he had a surprise. He took her to the planetarium at the Museum of Natural History."

"To see the stars," Leigh Ann say. "Oh my gosh. That is *so* romantic."

"Well, she certainly thought so," Elizabeth replies. "They were engaged a month later."

I rub my new pendant between my fingers. "St. Veronica. The stars," I mumble.

"What are you babbling about now?" Becca asks.

"I know what I have to do."

Chapter 27

In which order is restored to the universe

I'm forbidden to leave the apartment on Saturday until I prove to Mom that I am one hundred percent packed and ready to leave for France on Sunday morning. She has given me a list, and I take her through the piles of clothing on my bed, checking items off one by one. I can't help grinning at the sight of Dad's pen, wrapped in shiny red paper and tied up with silver ribbon, resting on top of my favorite denim jacket. He is going to love it!

"What's this?" she asks, pointing to a stack of five books, including a paperback of *The Count of Monte Cristo* that I've borrowed from Margaret—all fourteen hundred pages of it.

"Those are the books I'm taking."

"All of them? That's crazy. We're only going to be gone ten days. Even *you* cannot possibly need all these." She picks up a tattered copy of an old favorite, *Little Women.* "Sophie, you've read this ten times, I'll bet. Are you really going to read it again?"

"I don't know. Maybe. Sometimes I just need a little reminder of how important family is." I bat my eyelashes at her.

Unconvinced, she says, "Pick two."

I bite my lip, considering. "Four."

"Three."

"Okay," I say, returning the March sisters and a new, unread mystery to my bookshelves.

"Much more reasonable," says Mom, satisfied with our compromise. "I need you to run a few little errands for me, and then you're free for the rest of the day. Just stay out of jail, okay?"

"I'll try."

As soon as she's out of sight, I take *Little Women* off the shelf again and shove it into the bottom of my suitcase.

"Welcome back, Jo. You're finally going to see Paris."

At four o'clock, I arrive at the Hayden Planetarium, deep in the heart of that mysterious wilderness, the Upper West Side. One of the natives, a hopelessly-cute-but-apparently-clueless boy named Raf, waits for me outside the main entrance.

"It's about time," he says when I approach.

"Sorry. Slow bus. Really slow bus. Why don't you guys just move back over to the East Side? Think how much easier your life would be."

"That is not going to happen," he says. "Every day, my mom talks about how happy she is that she doesn't have to ride the six train anymore."

"Hey, we're going to have another subway— someday."

"Yeah, in, like, ten years. So, what's the big mystery? Why are we meeting here?"

"We're buying two tickets to the show inside the planetarium."

"Really? Cool. Believe it or not, I've never seen it."

"Um, yeah, you're still not going to, because the tickets aren't for us. Remember? We're supposed to meet Margaret and everybody at Perkatory at five o'clock. Do you listen to me at all?"

"Who?"

"Who? Who what? What are you talking about?"

"Who are the tickets for?"

"Oh. You'll see. Wait here—I'll just be a second." I leave him shivering in the quickly fading afternoon light as I go inside to the ticket window.

"Two adult tickets, please," I say, sliding my money across the counter.

I collect my change and start to head out the doors. I stop when I catch sight of Raf standing there, hands in his pockets, long hair blowing in the wind, knee-weakeningly cute.

"What is wrong with you, Sophie?" I say out loud,

feeling around my neck until I find my St. Veronica pendant. I squeeze it between my index finger and thumb and return to the ticket window.

"Hi, um, about children's tickets—that's for twelve and under, right?"

The woman blows a huge bubble with her gum. "Uh-huh."

After digging through my pockets, I throw every cent I have, change and all, on the counter, and add it up. I am thirty-five cents short. I glance back at Raf, who is looking at me and almost certainly wondering why the heck it is taking me so long to buy two tickets.

"That's all you got?" says the woman, who follows up her question with another bubble.

I nod. "Yeah, but I can—"

"I got it," she says, pushing the two tickets into my hand. "Merry Christmas."

"Thanks!" I say. "Merry Christmas to you, too!" Suddenly filled with enthusiasm, I skip out the door to Raf.

"Where were you?" he asks. "And how long are we gonna have to wait?"

"Not much longer," I say cheerfully.

Out on the street, a taxi stops and Gordon Winterbottom climbs out. He stands at the curb for a moment, reluctant to let the driver leave until he's sure that I'm really waiting for him at the entrance.

I can't help showing my surprise at the Gordon

Winterbottom who strolls down the sidewalk toward me with a definite spring in his step. He looks ten years younger than the guy who tormented me not so long ago. And somehow, in the three hours since Margaret and I told him the plan, he has bought a new navy-blue suit. It's the first time I've ever seen him in something that actually fits, and in a color other than drab brown.

"Wow, Mr. Winterbottom. You look great," I remark, straightening his tasteful red silk tie.

"Really? It looks all right? Not too . . . young?"

"Trust me. It is so much better," I say, sticking two of the tickets in his coat pocket. "Here you go."

He smiles nervously. "I hope this works."

I show him my crossed fingers.

Gordon taps Raf on the shoulder. "Young man, this one is a keeper," he says, pointing at me. "Whatever you do, don't let her get away."

Raf and I find ourselves in a blushing contest, and for once, I'm losing. His face is as red as Mr. Winterbottom's tie.

We're saved from further embarrassment when another taxi pulls up in front of the museum.

"There they are," I say. "Right on time."

"They?" Gordon inquires.

"Winnie and Elizabeth Harriman," I say. "That's how we got her out. She thinks she's going to tea with Elizabeth."

"You mean she doesn't know . . . ?"

Winnie steps out of the cab, followed by Elizabeth, who nudges her gently in our direction.

"She knows now," says Raf.

"Good luck," I say, taking Raf by the hand and leading him toward Elizabeth, who is holding her taxi.

The three of us watch from the curb as Winnie approaches Gordon. We can't hear what they're saying, but their body language tells us everything we need to know. After a few minutes of pleasant chatter, Gordon turns, tips an imaginary hat in our direction, and, with a hand placed at the small of Winnie's back, guides her into the planetarium.

"I can't believe it!" I cry. "It actually worked. Thank you, Elizabeth!"

"My pleasure," she says. "I love playing Cupid. Now, how about you two? Can I offer you a ride anywhere?"

Raf, who never turns down a free ride, is already halfway into the taxi when I pull him back by the arm.

"Thanks, Elizabeth, but we have . . . plans, here on the West Side."

"We do?" Raf asks, baffled. "I thought we were going to Perkatory."

"Slight change of plans," I say, winking at Elizabeth. "Don't worry, Raf. I'll let them know where we are. Eventually."

"Well, enjoy yourselves," she says, sliding into the backseat of the taxi. "And merry Christmas!"

The cab pulls away, leaving Raf and me standing there staring at each other.

"So . . . what are these mysterious plans?" he finally asks.

Grinning, I hold up the other two tickets. "You said you'd never been inside," I say. "No time like right now. C'mon."

We find two seats far away from Gordon and Winnie, who are too preoccupied with each other to see us come in, and wait for the "sunset" in the planetarium.

Raf squeezes my hand. "This was a really good idea."

"I know. I thought of it," I say.

"So, you're leaving tomorrow?"

"For ten days," I say as the dome turns purple, and then black, leaving our faces illuminated by a zillion stars sparkling above us.

I turn to see the expression on his face, but he's not looking at the stars.

He's looking at me.

We stay like that for a few seconds, and then he proves to me that maybe he's not so clueless, after all. He slips an arm around my shoulders and pulls me toward him. And then, right there in Hayden Planetarium, under Betelgeuse and Polaris, and Sirius and Arcturus, I finally get the kiss I've been waiting weeks for. It's the good-night kiss I didn't get, a Christmas kiss, and my New Year's kiss all rolled into one.

As we sit there, lips still just inches apart, my phone buzzes. It's a text from Margaret:

Where are you?

I text back:

I'll be a little late.
I'm seeing stars.

Chapter 28

A few final words, from somewhere over the Atlantic

Twenty-four hours later, I'm in the window seat on the flight to Paris with Jane Austen's *Emma* on my lap and still thinking about those stars. As I start to nod off, though, my mind runs through the events of the past few months. Way back in September, I didn't even know Leigh Ann, and now she's like a sister, along with Margaret and Becca. Livvy, soon to be the newest member of the Blazers, was anything but a friend. I'd never heard of Malcolm Chance or Elizabeth Harriman, or Gordon Winterbottom, and Raf and I were . . . well, just friends. Okay, technically, as far as my parents are concerned, that hasn't changed, but, well . . . you know.

So, where to from here? I wonder as I gaze out the window at the deep blue sky and the ocean below. I smile, remembering the promise I made to my mom on the way home from Bartleman's the night of the auction. Not to worry, Mom. After the events of the past few days, I believe—more than ever—that life really is one amazing adventure after another.

With New Year's Day just around the corner, I can't help wondering what surprises my thirteenth year will bring. What lies over the horizon for me and the rest of the Red Blazer Girls?

I can't wait to find out.

Acknowledgments

In the three years since the first Red Blazer Girls book, *The Ring of Rocamadour,* hit the bookstore shelves, I've learned a great deal about the world of children's book publishing. In short, it is a wonderful place, full of talented, committed, and very hardworking people who love and believe in books as much as I do. I would like to extend heartfelt thanks and appreciation to everyone who has been a part of my little adventure, with special recognition going to:

Kate Gartner, for your playful, creative design work on all four RBG books. I love the way they look!

Daniel Baxter, for those terrific covers and interior illustrations, and the portrait of Isabel and Maggie that makes me smile every time I look at it.

All the sales, publicity, and marketing folks at Random House Children's Books, for your enthusiastic and continuous support of my books.

Rebecca Waugh at Listening Library and Tai Alexandra Ricci, the voice of Sophie, for the great audiobook versions of the RBGs.

Copy editors Artie Bennett, Jenny Golub, Sue Cohan, and Janet Renard, for their patience, diligence, and tenacity.

My agent, Rosemary Stimola, for believing in "the girls" from the very beginning.

My editor, Nancy Hinkel, who has a knack for making exactly the right suggestion at exactly the right moment in exactly the right way. It's a gift, really.

Readers, friends, librarians, and fans of "the girls": Thanks for all the nice things you've said about Sophie and her friends!

As always, my friends and family, especially LLG.

. . . and a tip of the metaphorical cap to David Levithan and Rachel Cohn's brilliant book *Dash & Lily's Book of Dares*.

About the Author

Michael D. Beil's first Red Blazer Girls installment, *The Ring of Rocamadour,* was an Edgar Allan Poe Award Nominee for Best Children's Mystery. He has published three more books about the Red Blazer Girls since then: *The Vanishing Violin, The Mistaken Masterpiece,* and *The Secret Cellar.* He is also the author of *Summer at Forsaken Lake.*

Mr. Beil, who teaches English and helms the theater program at a New York City high school, has, in his own words, "too many hobbies to count." When he's not teaching or writing, he loves reading, skiing, sailing, cooking, playing cello, and hiking—including climbing Mount Kilimanjaro. He finds literary inspiration in everything from classic films to Charles Dickens to that beloved barrister, Horace Rumpole.

He and his wife, Laura Grimmer, share their Manhattan home with dogs Isabel and Maggie and cats Cyril and Emma.

Also by Michael D. Beil